NEVER PICK A PRETTY WOMAN
By
Mary M. Forbes

BOOK ONE: Crystal Ridge Series

NEVER PICK A PRETTY WOMAN

Copyright 2014: Mary M. Forbes
ISBN No.: 13: 978-1499584622
          10: 1499584628

All rights reserved. No part of this book may be used or reproduced in any manner whatsoever without the written permission from the publisher or author, except in the brief quotations embodied in critical articles and/or reviews.

Forbes Publications
E-mail: marymforbes49@yahoo.ca
Website: http://marymforbes.wordpress.com

NEVER PICK A PRETTY WOMAN

Chapter One

A green-eyed monster, often named jealousy reared its' ugly head with a vengeance. Sophie Donnelly watched in shock as her fiancée, Dennis leaned towards the woman beside him. Sophie barely felt the heavy thud as Pat, her best friend, barreled into her back. They were just exiting the washroom. The lights were dim. She rubbed her eyes. Opening them she could see no difference.

No – no way. Not possible. The only man who ever asked for her hand in marriage sat kissing Liz. Dennis's face wasn't visible. But Liz, completely involved, had her eyes closed and her flushed face told the story. Dennis's hand tangled with Liz's hair, pulling her closer. He definitely wasn't pushing her away.

Humiliation, hurt and anger rushed in simultaneously. The raucous crowd at Ranchman's on a Friday night during Stampede week became muted. Sights blurred, a swirl of color as though Sophie rode on a merry-go-round, spinning out of control crossed in front of her vision.

She moaned and turning to the entrance, fled. Knocking against people she kept her eyes glued to the dusty floor. Like brambles in a forest, people clawed and barked at her.

"Sophie, wait. Sophie, find out-" Pat, following her, tried to grab her arm. Sophie flung it away. Of course Pat would say that. Dennis, Pat's brother didn't ever do much wrong in Pat's eyes. A clear thought penetrated. Obviously loyalty belonged first to family, not best friends. Sophie didn't understand. She had no siblings.

Dennis neglecting Sophie to pay Liz his full attention for over a month, now kissed her. Dennis was engaged to her and should not be kissing another woman.

Outside, for once she didn't laugh at the sign *'have a beer with your dog'*. She didn't notice all the posters, mainly advertising, but looking like wanted posters on the wooden walls. She could still hear voices and laughter above the loud music. The tiered patio, packed with gyrating, loud bodies remained the same as when they arrived. Sophie started to run to the back towards the car. Tears blurred her eyes. The narrow, uneven entrance lane caused her to stumble, nearly falling. She discarded her high-heel sandals with ease. In her bare-feet she touched the pebbles and possibly glass pressing into her feet, but didn't care. Humiliation and disbelief remained foremost on her mind. Dennis, after chasing her for as long as she recollected, was now kissing another woman – one short month before their wedding.

  She stopped abruptly when she realized she was heading towards Dennis's car. She wasn't going into his car to wait for the cheating bastard. Turning she went back to the darkness away from the front patio and entrance to the north side of the building. The narrow exit lane was uneven as well. She slowed to a limping walk. Her feet refused to adjust to this punishment anymore. She had probably ruined her pedicure and she dwelled on that tragic event, hoping to alleviate the agony of betrayal.

  Plopping down on the wooden boardwalk on the south side of the building, she was finally alone. Only dark logs, with no windows were behind. She concentrated on the throb in her feet. The sounds were subdued. She heard the traffic murmur on McLeod Trail. A cool and gentle breeze brushed her arms. Her skimpy pink t-shirt no longer looked right in the cooling evening. But people said she looked sexy and that seemed important. She didn't understand why or when being fashionable became so significant. Again mundane thoughts pushed to the front and she grasped onto them with determined tenacity but failed.

  Confusion ran rampant throughout her brain. What could she do? She was part owner of their business, she lived with Dennis, and worst of all she no longer had a vehicle.

Just another idea Dennis had to save money. More like control she realized in retrospect. It was his way of having her rely on him for her every need. Trap might be the right word. She understood like a wild animal might, she was ensnared with nowhere to run. Panic set in swiftly with clammy hands and gasps for air when she thought of her situation. She started panting. She stared down at her former perfect pink pedicure, concentrating on the polish glinting in the dim light. Her toes did appear nice, if they weren't so badly chipped. She needed a touch-up on her toes. Why was she barefoot? Unwanted memories seeped in. She tried to take a deep breath. Then another.

The tears came out in long, hard gulps and she was helpless to stop them. Leaning into her cupped hands against her sides, she rocked back and forth. The sky above was remote with cold, glassy stars and she wanted to howl her despair to the moon. What was she going to do? Her job, her fiancée, her apartment and probably her best friend all lost in one moment.

Her phone dinged. Once, twice... She debated even looking at it. Astonishment replaced hurt. Dennis had texted her? She looked at the message. *'It's not what it looks like.'* It's not? How was she interpreting the scene wrong? When she came out of Ranchman's washroom she saw Dennis, her fiancée, kissing Liz. Simple and precise and easily read wasn't it?

Her phone dinged again. Perhaps he was ready to tell her what it really was he was doing. Maybe giving Liz CPR? But this time Pat texted her. *'Come back and let him explain.'* Explain? Dennis, kissing Liz. What was to explain? Disgust with herself mostly for being such a fool made Sophie glance at the phone, then nearly toss it into the next door lot. It was obvious she and Dennis were not suited, so why had they perpetuated this farce for so long? Why had she meekly let him rule and control her life? She did not love Dennis and for all his chasing since high-school, Dennis didn't love her. She knew that. Now that the truth became a fact, it hurt.

She looked around unable to focus, still unsure what she would do. A steady pounding in her ears joined with pain across the back of her head. As she realized her situation, gloom invaded again. What was she going to do?

She cupped her face in her hands, elbows digging into her upper legs and rocked. Her legs and arms trembled. Surely something would come to her. Then it did. She wanted to go back home. She wanted to see her mom. Her mom, her only real true friend, would have the right answers. Her mom would help her.

She sensed a presence beside her. Someone crouched nearby. Somebody brushed her arm with a hand. But she dared not look, so sure it would be Dennis. Dennis must never realize how much he hurt her. She couldn't give him that satisfaction. Besides she might well start punching that smug know-it-all face.

"What can I do to help you?"

Her head whipped around and her green eyes widened in shock. This wasn't Dennis. This apparition appeared to be a cowboy in her dreams. His eyes were narrowed, sultry and dark with long black lashes to match his short dark hair. A cowboy hat was tilted back to reveal his incredible features. His eyes suddenly widened in surprise when he saw her face, then dropped to the ground. He swore. Perplexed, she wanted to ask him what that was about. Before she had the chance, she noticed he was dangling the straps of her sandals with one finger.

"Prince Charming?" Light banter slipped easily inside. Something familiar and calming.

"You want your shoes back little princess?" He smiled. It took her a moment to compose herself. His smile was breathtaking and vaguely familiar. Had she met him somewhere? No, surely she would remember if she had.

She took the offered shoes silently and leaned over to put them on again. The bottom of her feet stung. She kept her head bent so this man couldn't see her face. Her mascara was probably streaked, leaving black marks all over her face. Why did that matter?

Her priority should be what to do with Dennis, not start a new relationship. She recognized the expression in the stranger's eyes. All men had that look for a short period of time. Over an interval a subtle change would occur. Men lost interest in pursuing her and moved on. Or worse, they became controlling jerks. Usually it was flattering to have a guy flirt with her. Eventually she realized none remained long enough to know her. Most men wanted to be seen with her in public or have a short fling. Only Dennis had remained steadfast since high-school and she always believed Dennis to be her rock. Now, he acted bored, like all the others.

That brought her circumstances back to haunt her. She dropped her head into her palms. Her sobs shook her body, intense and real. Trust dissipated in self-condemnation. Why did everyone, now even Dennis, abandon her? What was she doing wrong?

"I want my mommy." She moaned, still rocking. Her arms wrapped around to cradle her stomach. Her mother, the only person she had left in the world.

"Do you want me to take you to your mom?" The man stood abruptly, towering above her. She looked up and tried to smile. Heavy gulps erupted involuntarily from her lips.

"She's way out in Crystal Ridge." Sophie shook her head and looked down to study the pit marks and cracked potholes in the pavement with intensity. Shadows and light played on the surface as the huge Ranchman's sign up front, flashed its' red signal. She wanted to block the hurt and anger out. Sometimes concentrating elsewhere helped.

When she looked up, she attempted another smile. "Can you drive me to the bus station?"

She wouldn't go with Dennis in his new BMW. She wasn't going back into their Four Plus Incorporated offices and let anyone make snide, allegedly sympathetic remarks to her. And she definitely wasn't going back to the apartment she and Dennis shared.

"Crystal Ridge," The man gave a short laugh. "That's where I'm from."

"I'm sure you're not." Sophie shook her head as she studied him. She thanked God for the distraction numbing the pain. Crystal Ridge was a small town. She was quite sure she'd never seen anyone who looked remotely like this guy. "I grew up there and I should know. I never saw you before."

"Well, I don't live right in town anymore, but I used to. I bought the old Dawson place a few years back," the man continued with a slight smile on his perfectly shaped lips.

Oh he was gorgeous and unlike any boy or man she'd seen in Crystal Ridge. Yet he said he lived there. Confusion penetrated her thoughts.

"Okay." She nodded, not wanting to argue.

It had been a few years since she'd been there, other than short visits to see her mom. Those visits had nearly stopped too. Dennis decided they would get rid of her car. They lived and worked together, so why would she possibly need a car? Without her own vehicle she was lucky if they went to Crystal Ridge for Christmas. When had her life become so busy she didn't even have time for her mother? She recalled her mother mentioning Butch Dawson had died.

"Are you riding at the Stampede?"

"I'm not riding. I just lent a buddy my horse. He's an outrider in the chuck-wagon races." He was very tall. He reached down to help her stand. And he kept holding her hand. Warmth seeped inside. He was very calm and comforting.

"You know you're *still* the most beautiful woman I've ever seen." He was studying her very carefully now. She was drawn to his steady gaze and felt somewhat weak.

Should she say something? Those exact words were said many, many times before. What good did it do her, to be good-looking? Dennis made her realize it was a liability, not an asset. Goodness gracious, she was even thinking like him. She wondered if there was a preconceived idea of what beautiful people might be. This man should know. Talk about stunning.

"But obviously I'm not very likable."

"How do you know it's your fault?" His breath was a whisper close to her lips. Was he going to kiss her? He was going to kiss her. "Maybe it's his fault."

It started, an undemanding comfort kiss and shouldn't be evoking this longing deep within her body. It was soothing being held in his solid arms. She leaned in and soaked up his strength she needed so badly. She wasn't sure who deepened the kiss but realized her arms encircled his neck and his hands cupped her face. His lips moved over hers first brushing softly, then became persuasive, until she opened her mouth to answer his demand. The pressure was divine and for a moment she forgot she was heart-broken. She moved her hands to his muscled back, drawing him closer. His heat was intense, tantalizing against her chest. Her new cowboy sure knew how to kiss, so much better than Dennis.

"You fickle bitch!"

Chapter Two

Sophie snapped back, trying to clear her glazed eyes. *My-oh my, what a wonderful day.* Her mood immediately dampened when she saw Dennis standing there. Dennis yelling at her, calling her names? Embarrassment mingled with confusion. She would never kiss a stranger. She remembered the reason she kissed a stranger and guilt fled.

A nervous chuckle escaped and she clasped her hands over her lips. Avoiding Dennis, she watched the stranger instead. He moved back looking composed and unruffled. So much for a kiss to end all kisses. His eyes glinted in the dim light. A slight smile curved his sensuous lips. He looked ready to laugh as well.

"You're laughing at me." Dennis snapped, loud and clear.

She reluctantly turned to Dennis. He appeared astounded. With his impeccable suit, well groomed and puffed up, Dennis looked like a rooster and not intimidating even as he clenched his fists. He watched Sophie, not the cowboy. She wondered if he was going to hit her. Her breath caught in her throat. She winced and stepped back.

"No, I laughed at your words. Fickle? What the hell does that mean?" Sophie stated vigorously. Dennis, often cruel with cutting words that injured, was never physical threatening before today. Her chin jutted out with false courage. He acted as though she'd betrayed him. Upon reflection, that was normal. He blamed her for every problem they had. "In fact Dennis, my darling, you can go to hell. It shouldn't matter what I'm doing. You made that perfectly clear when you kissed Liz."

"I told you it wasn't what it looked like. She. . ."

"I don't care what happened. I'm leaving. We're through." Sophie refused to falter.

"We can talk more when we get home. Come on. The others can catch a cab." Dennis reached for her arm. His face filled with stiff condemnation. He turned to glare at the strange man. Dennis was all ruffle and false banter. The man must have known that. He gave a small chuckle, standing his ground.

Sophie wanted to giggle again. Dennis grabbed her arm. Sophie yanked away, stepping further back. "Don't touch me."

"I'm not going home." She fought to appear casual. Dennis would never see how much he wounded her. Let him believe she was shallow and unfeeling like he always claimed. Much better he thought that than him knowing how much he'd hurt her. For many years, safe and secure, she could always rely on Dennis. But he was not the reliable, trustworthy man she believed he was.

Dennis reached out again to grab her arm. This time the man stepped between them, still saying nothing. Dennis's arm dropped. He was quite a bit smaller than the cowboy. After a moment Dennis grunted and turned, muttering as he walked away. It all happened so fast, Sophie had trouble assimilating it.

"What's your name?" Sophie gave a short mortified laugh. "He's never seen me kissing strange men before."

"Jake, Jake McCallum and I'm not exactly a stranger." The cowboy reached up and tipped his hat. "And you are Sophie, Sophie Donnelly unless that's changed. You didn't marry him did you?"

She looked up at him with suspicion. She still couldn't place who he might be. "I can't remember you." She reached up to cover her mouth. Why did she always blurt out without thinking? Was that an insult? Concentrate as she might, she couldn't summon him up in her mind.

"I see how memorable I am," Jake was still smiling.

"I'm sorry. My mind is going blank. I'll probably remember when…"

"I was older than you and you probably paid me no mind. You were a very popular girl in high-school I recall." Jake had his slow, sexy smile in place, but his eyes seemed dejected. Why?

"Are you sure you can drive me?" Sophie asked, trying to ignore the sadness. There were lots of people she'd forgotten. It was over twelve years since she'd left Crystal Falls. But this guy… oh wow. She looked back up at his breath-taking face. It seemed impossible she would have forgotten him

His eyes lightened to a twinkle. His lips opened in a wide, playful grin. "Any time you…"

Sophie realized what she insinuated and interrupted. "I meant can you drive me home." She flushed and her eyes dropped to the ground. How disconcerting.

"Glad you clarified that. My heart skipped a beat for a second. " Jake's tone was bright. He nodded. "I was about to go out there anyway. It's really no big deal."

"Did I know you well?"

"I thought so." He was noncommittal and appeared unconcerned. "Come on, let's get you home."

She looked around the parking-lot, wondering what kind of vehicle he drove. She had a strong urge to run away from him right now. She might have lost her instincts along with her fiancée. Could Jake be a danger to her? Something said he might be, not in a scary way though. She didn't understand why. Her head, still buzzing, her mind, a chaotic mixture of confusion refused to focus. She might be getting a cold. Stiff and achy, she wondered if she wasn't just stuffed up from too much crying. She resented every tear she shed over Dennis.

Jake took her elbow and guided her over to a fully loaded silver Silverado. She whistled, smiling and oddly happy to see he drove a truck. Cowboys didn't drive BMW's like Dennis. He was the polar opposite of Dennis and that was good. Her experience, long ago said cowboys didn't pose a danger to anyone.

   The night sky, clear with stars, had a full moon shining across the fields. The city lights dissolved into the country sky. They headed south from Calgary. Barren hills sparkled as though the stars had dropped to the ground. After they turned off the main highway and drove a bit, the hills started getting larger, more trees and forests covered them. The sky dome didn't look as dominating. The moon filtered through ebony laced branches. Everything appeared silver and charcoal. Beautiful and quiet, the two-lane road was soon tree-lined, dark and mysterious like a tunnel. At the top of a hill, she saw the sky with fluffy clouds now, causing moonlight to appear hazy. Almost immediately they would drop back into a valley and darkness would cover the land again.
   They were both silent. It wasn't an uncomfortable silence. She mulled over her options. And the harder she concentrated, the more confused she became. Should she throw everything away because Dennis kissed Liz? Yes whispered throughout and the cause wasn't because of the kiss. She looked for an excuse to cancel the wedding. She smiled, imagining Dennis's fury over the money they had deposited for the special event. Uneasiness settled inside. Her thoughts weren't nice. But she should feel grateful for that kiss, instead of pining over it. It was a close call.
   Some people might find Dennis's 'take charge' attitude appealing. Even though there were four owners at Four Plus, Dennis bossed everyone around. At first it hadn't bothered her, being as he had business administration and management courses. But now she didn't find his personality appealing. Dennis smothered her, not ever letting her make a decision on her own. Inside, a niggling hurt persisted. Her pride suffered. Dennis preferred Liz over her and why? Liz drab and mousy, didn't appear lively or entertaining. And neither did Dennis.

Remorse crept inside. Perhaps Dennis realized she found him boring, drab and mousy.

Her thoughts moved to Pat. Pat was her best friend. She wanted to cry then. She tried to reason it out. She would always consider Pat her friend and now Pat must decide. Rawness, hurt and bitterness made her push her thoughts away.

She listened to the hum of the air-conditioner. Jake was silent too as he kept his eyes on the road ahead. She wanted the wind to blow her troubles away. The breeze would help her be light and carefree again. Wind would blow the heavy brick lying on her chest far away.

"Can I roll down the window?" She asked in the silence.

Her mother would be horrified. Her riding with a strange man was a definite no-no to her mother. To top it all off, they were now in the middle of nowhere. Yet, she wasn't afraid. No, he said he wasn't a stranger. He was from Crystal Ridge and she didn't remember him. But Crystal Ridge didn't have all nice people either.

"Sure," Jake leaned over and turned the air-conditioner off. "It gets kind of stale doesn't it?"

They both rolled down their windows and almost by instinct the truck sped up. It was like being a teen again, untroubled and unrestricted. Jake broke the silence and his words startled her.

"I shouldn't have kissed you."

The last thing Sophie was interested in was coming back to reality. She enjoyed the breeze on her face and the way the wind was blowing everything from her mind.

"And you came to that conclusion just now?" She asked sarcastically, heart sinking.

First Dennis, now Jake both rejected her. Her self-esteem plummeted further into a deep, dark hole. Everyone believed she had it so easy. Guys swarmed around her like flies. But reality was so different. Guys liked to flirt with her but no guy wanted to see the real Sophie Donnelly. Her outer shell was what they all saw, nothing more.

Then she wanted to take her words back. Jake, without hesitation, helped her when everyone else failed her. To her knowledge they'd never been close friends and he owed her nothing. She was being rude to him.

But he just smiled, that slow sexy smile "Strong back and weak mind?"

She flushed. She had often claimed she wanted just that as a joke, when she was going to school. Jake must have heard her. "Men like that did appear less trouble. Did I ever say that to you?"

"I heard you say it a few times, but never directed towards me." Jake slowed his truck to maneuver a corner. "I heard you tell Dennis he was too smart for you too. Why become engaged to him? Is he really too smart for you?"

"I thought I loved him, but it's just an illusion. I worked so hard, there wasn't time to meet others." Sophie stiffened when she realized what she was about to say. Jake knew way too much about her to be a stranger. Did she give the impression she needed a man and any man would do? That's what her words sounded like to her.

"Dennis was a smart-ass from what I saw. He was always a bad one for looking down his nose at us poor peons. Maybe because his dad manages the bank?" Jake gave a chuckle but it sounded bitter. "I thought you had no use for him either."

"He was such a know it all. Dennis was hard to like." Sophie clamped her hands over her mouth. It wasn't nice to be so nasty. "Were you a poor peon Jake?"

"According to Dennis we all were." Jake shook his head, not answering the question directly. "So I take it you don't want a man to be too smart?"

"There are problems when dealing with overly intelligent people." Sophie slanted him a cheeky grin. She enjoyed their silly banter much more than being serious. It was better than facing reality, the reality of knowing Dennis always considered her dumb.

"If it's lack of intelligence you're looking for, I'm definitely your man." His deep voice had a teasing lilt. She laughed.

At least Jake had a sense of humor, something she realized Dennis didn't have or at least he never showed her that side of his nature. In high-school, twelve years past, both her and Pat realized that about Dennis, even as teens. Dennis would tell them what to do and they, being teenagers would do the exact opposite whenever possible. Dennis, so intense and serious never smiled much. He appeared old-fashioned in his strict tone and stiff behavior. It was one of the reasons she'd ignored his love-struck puppy eyes throughout high-school. She should have listened to her inner voice. Dennis wasn't much fun. And Dennis obviously liked the fact she was dumb as well. Much easier to manipulate her. Why did it take her so long to realize that?

"How old are you?" She was still trying to place Jake instead. Better to concentrate on him, then Dennis. Dennis was the past and Sophie hated dwelling on the past.

"I'm thirty-five. Long out of high-school when you started." Jake's jaw clenched. "I doubt you ever noticed me."

"Why did you kiss me then?" It was time to change the subject. Who was he? Had she kissed him before? No, she would have considered Jake old in those days probably.

"I wanted to, but we shouldn't always just give into our wants?" She groaned. He sounded serious. She did not want serious.

"What's the harm? Are you married Jake?" Her voice hardened. She had seen many times, being married didn't stop some men from playing around.

"I'm not married Sophie." His tone was light. "There's no *harm* in kissing you. Just a little concern, that's all. I need to concentrate on my ranch more than I need a lover in my life now."

"You think a simple kiss would turn into us being lovers?" Was Jake conceited? Now he really had her thinking. Who was he? She tried to think of all the playboys in school. Jake's face didn't pop into her mind.

"There was a time-" Jake's voice dropped off. "But, no Sophie we can't be lovers."

They topped a hill and through the evergreens she saw a little lights flickering. Those few twinkling lights looked comforting. The huge cliff, or crystal ridge, they all called it, was hidden in the dimness of night. When the sun was shining in the mornings, it was breath-taking. Light glinted off quartz. They often rode through 'no-man's land'. As teens it was a perfect spot to make out. The police, nor many adults ever seemed to go there. They called it 'no man's land' because no one appeared to own it. Perhaps the town did. Shorty, the rancher to the south of town didn't own it. And neither Dawson nor the Donnelly ranches to the north owned it either.

She started to describe where her mother lived, hoping her mother was still up. She just never thought things through. If her mom was sleeping would her arrival frighten her?

"I know where Alice Donnelly lives."

"Of course you do." She nodded. "We're neighbors. Do you still live in Dawson shack or have you built a new house?" The shack was a short distance from the Donnelly house.

"Yeah, I still live in the shack. Haven't had time to change that." Jake nodded. "So we're close neighbors for sure."

The idea of having sexy Jake McCallum for a neighbor was intriguing. The Dawson shack was less than a half-mile away. The exciting prospect of trying to convince Jake he could pursue a romantic interlude and build a ranch was an intriguing challenge.

Nibbling on her bottom lip she knew she was a bitch. Pictures of Dennis crossed her mind. His sandy hair and smoky eyes were attractive but the thin, disapproving line of his mouth took away the appeal. And she couldn't banish that stern expression from her mind. But still, she was ready to marry him a few weeks away. Perhaps she was fickle because she sure sounded shallow.

She pushed all her worries to the back of her mind. Tonight she wanted to get away from Dennis. Tomorrow she would worry about her future and what to do about Jake.

The house, old and sprawling sat amongst the pines. It had a neglected appearance to it now her dad had passed away. But it looked pretty and welcoming in the headlights. The house was log and her mother maintained flower gardens all around the yard. Everything was in full bloom. Across the front, a verandah with potted geraniums and hanging petunias fought with the paint chipped boards. Truly it was the most beautiful sight she'd ever seen.

Alice greeted them at the door. The startled expression on her face changed to joy as she gave Sophie a comforting hug. Then she turned to the man standing behind Sophie.

"Jake, what are you doing here with Sophie?"

Chapter Three

"I just drove Sophie home," Jake mumbled, a child caught in the act of doing something wrong. He was scowling. His eyes darted to Sophie's face, then back to Alice.

"You were in Calgary?" Alice continued, looking somewhat confused herself. "I thought you'd be out celebrating with Tracy tonight."

"Celebrating? Why?"

"Well, she told me in the grocery store this afternoon you two were engaged. Congratulations by the way." Alice pulled Sophie c oser, away from Jake.

"She told you that? Are you sure?" Jake expression appeared puzzled, but he didn't deny the engagement Sophie noticed.

"I'm sure. I'm not going senile yet Jake." Alice continued.

The light from the living-room lamp poured into the small entrance hall, creating shadows on the three faces. Jake shrugged, turning to the door.

Sophie looked at her mother mystified. Once again she felt lost and floundering for air. Jake and Tracy? Tracy Phillips? It wasn't possible. There must be another Tracy in town.

"We all want to know when we can expect to hear wedding bells."

No wonder Jake said he shouldn't have kissed her. Now, he stood silent and awkward, saying nothing.

"I'll see you out." Surely he understood why her voice might be cool. She wanted to know why he shouldn't kiss her and now that she heard, she didn't want to know. Which was odd. She had just met Jake.

He had the decency to blush. He nodded his head and turned to walk out the door. At the door he held the door open, as though wanting to say something. He remained silent.

"Thanks for the ride Jake," Sophie made every attempt to keep her voice nonchalant. He nodded politely but didn't look at her.

After closing the door, she turned to her mother. "Tracy? You mean Tracy Phillips, the girl voted most likely to be a spinster?"

"Don't be so nasty, Sophie. It's not like you. Yes, it's Tracy Phillips." Her mother grabbed her hand and led her into the dimly lit living room. The TV was blaring. She pushed Sophie down, then went over to turn the TV off. She came to sit beside Sophie on the sofa.

Alice was a plump, older version of Sophie. Her auburn hair was streaked with grey and her vivid green eyes had wrinkles she called laughter lines around the edges. Sophie was so glad to see her mother's familiar face. But she felt at odds, disoriented.

Jake and Tracy. Sophie couldn't grasp that reality. Regardless of how often Sophie tried to talk to her Tracy met all conversations with offensive belligerence. Tracy didn't trust anyone who tried to be friendly. After a time, she realized it was best to just avoid Tracy. Tracy had a big chip on her shoulder— *Tracy against the world*. She couldn't imagine a cowboy finding Tracy appealing. But how could she judge? Love made strange bed partners. Oh yuck, that conjured up a vision she didn't want. And a feeling akin to possessiveness flooded her veins. Sophie was jealous of Tracy Phillips? How ludicrous was that?

Why now would Tracy trust Jake enough to become engaged? As far as Sophie could recall Tracy never dated anyone in high-school. Jake wasn't talkative, but he seemed so kind and willing to help, surely traits Tracy would scoff at.

"Where's Dennis. And what were you doing with Jake?" Her mother cut right to the chase and her words broke Sophie's thoughts. Dennis? Oh yeah Dennis, her no longer fiancée.

Because this was her mother, the only person she could trust unconditionally, Sophie burst into tears. She sat on her mother's brightly flowered couch as her mother gathered her into her arms. "Oh mom, I caught Dennis kissing Liz. She's the new acccuntant we hired."

"And what were you doing with Jake?" Her mother pushed on.

"He was there at Ranchman's and when I told him I wanted to go home, he offered to drive me and that's all."

"Are you sure?" Her mother sighed. "I know you Sophie. Were you flirting with Jake when Dennis kissed the accountant?"

"Mom!" Sophie was surprised at Alice's insinuation. "You're just like Pat, thinking it's my fault. No I was not. Jake came to talk to me after, when I went outside."

Her heart sank into depression. She had made a mistake, coming home. It was time to reassess her whole personality. It appeared everyone thought she was just this flighty, self-centered person including her own mother. She wasn't was she? Her head hurt from trying to think what she could do. She couldn't go to the apartment she and Dennis shared. She flushed. Her mother didn't know that. Would it matter? Would her mother say something like since they were *'living in sin'* they should make it right? "For your information I was coming out of the washroom at Ranchman's with Pat, not flirting with anyone."

"I'm sorry. I wasn't saying it was your fault." Alice looked sad as she threw her arms around Sophie, rocking her. "My too beautiful little girl. Life isn't always as easy for beautiful people as some think. Dennis was not right for you anyway."

Just like Jake isn't right for Tracy, she wanted to say, but didn't. She didn't know Jake. She only knew what he looked like and that was on her mind, not Dennis's betrayal.

"That's the first time you said that to me. Why didn't you tell me before I got engaged? You would have let me marry him without telling me?"

"You wouldn't listen to me anyway," Alice said lightly, stroking her arms. "You really aren't heartbroken, because you know this already. You loved Dennis like a brother. Why on earth did you become engaged to him? You wouldn't give him the time of day here when you were going to school."

"We were just so busy. There was never any time... He asked me and..." Sophie's voice trailed off.

It was the second time her thoughts swayed in this direction. So she accepted Dennis just because there was no other guy around? It was all baffling. Dennis kissing Liz didn't bother her nearly as much as Jake's kissing her and then finding out he belonged to Tracy. What was wrong? Dennis's betrayal hurt her pride. Dennis had always worshipped her and it was visible to everyone. His choosing another woman after all this time didn't seem real. If she couldn't trust Dennis she doubted she could trust anyone.

"What about the business? I thought it was going so well. You are going to continue with your business, aren't you?" Alice interrupted her thoughts. "I'm so proud of you. When you were young I didn't think you'd ever stick with anything. But you ended up working for ten years at the same job. It was such a relief to know you were growing up."

"I know," Sophie smiled through her tears. Her mother was right.

From deciding to be a rancher, or raising race-horses, to being a fashion designer or interior decorator, she couldn't make up her mind throughout high-school. Why had she settled on website designing?

Was she happy there? And she had to answer honestly, at least to herself, no. Although she liked the designing part she wasn't happy working day and night, going home with Dennis and having to cater to his wishes or decisions. He was always too tired to go anywhere except work unless they were meeting clients. Dennis was very boring. Dennis was a young version of his father. Mr. Willows was the bank manager in town. Stuffy and serious, she doubted he had ever smiled or enjoyed anything but numbers. And his son was just the same. Why hadn't she thought things through instead of ramming ahead?

"Mom. I'm not going back to the office. It would be so humiliating to watch Dennis and Liz. Besides I gave up my apartment and was living with…" She flushed. Her mother could be so old-fashioned at times.

She studied the fireplace instead. It was too hot for a fire now, but she could recall the times she and Alice curled up on the couches to watch a movie or read books, so cozy and comfortable. The times Alice would bring in hot chocolate and cookies would always mean security, especially when she felt so empty and lost after her dad passed away. How could her mother be so strong?

"I knew you two were living together. I told you to wait until you're married." Alice stated lightly. "I'm not that bad am I? You could have told me. It is a problem you have no place to stay in Calgary and you work with him, I agree."

"So what should I do?"

"Why don't you take a few weeks off and decide? I don't work the ranch anymore but we'll find something to do. I lease the land to Jake now."

Sophie was very angry at herself, the way her heart leapt up when she heard his name. "Why are you leasing the land?"

"It's all too much work for me. It's hard to find reliable people and Jake is reliable. But he didn't want to just work for me." Alice sighed. "Sophie, Tracy told me this afternoon in the grocery store she and Jake are engaged."

"I don't see where that's my problem," Sophie flushed, looking down at the scarred hardwood floor her mother still polished to a shine.

"I can see the way you look at Jake and the way he looked at you for that matter." Alice rubbed her hand down Sophie's arm in a soothing gesture. "I taught you better. You don't go after someone else's man. If Jake is interested in you, he'll break the engagement."

"I have no interest in Jake mom. And if he's engaged to Tracy I won't interfere." Sophie protested, perhaps a little too vehemently. She rubbed her nose just in case it was growing. "When did Jake come to Crystal Ridge and do you know why?"

Her mother looked at her oddly. "You can't remember Jake McCallum?"

Jake. Finally faint niggling memories entered her mind. Poor, serious Jake McCallum who looked after his drunken father. The McCallum's were poor as church-mice. Angus McCallum beat his son and neglected him, or so the rumor went. No one seemed to know for sure. Now Jake seemed so far from the solemn, quiet boy he used to be. Well, in retrospect he was still very quiet. And his sweet smile was still there.

He had rarely talked to her, that sad, skinny boy. But he always smiled when she saw him and she recalled she loved that smile even then. He spent most his time at the Dawson ranch. Occasionally they crossed paths when she was out riding. His smile made her feel as though she was the only person in the world.

Jake was five years older than her. By the time she started high-school he was out of school. A light flickered in her mind. Now it made sense, Jake with Dawson's ranch. Rarely found in town, it was rumored Jake spent all his time on the ranch working. Not that she'd paid much mind then. Jake was too old and Randy, Crystal Ridge's upcoming hockey star was much more interesting at the time.

Then her last encounter with Jake hit her with a wham. Mortification and embarrassment flooded inside. No wonder she wanted to suppress the memory. She agreed to let him come riding with her when he asked. Sometimes his intense gaze made her uncomfortable but he rarely showed her that look. That day they went riding to Crystal Ridge, the teen make-out, site. But Jake wasn't a teen. Jake was a man.

With most the teen boys pursuing her, would a man feel the same? Curiosity overcame hesitation when they stopped beneath the ridge.

"Jake will you kiss me?" With the boldness of a seventeen year old Sophie was ripe to explore the effect she had on men. Jake seemed like a willing candidate. He was older, but still young enough to flirt with. Sophie loved playing, just to see a man's reaction.

"Someday Sophie." Jake hesitated, then looked up. He appeared in pain. His dark eyes were burning with something she didn't understand. "Today, be a good girl and behave yourself. You have Randy to kiss."

"Where's Randy?" She tried desperately to erase the memory.

Jake rejected her then and tonight he had again. Three times she had been rejected. And tonight it was Jake's second time.

Her mother laughed. "Oh my little Sophie. Can you hold a thought for more than a moment? Randy is in Calgary, married to some girl he met there. Do you care?"

"No. Randy and I were pretty well finished by the time we got out of high-school." Sophie laughed too, feeling better.

"Didn't Jake's mother take off with the mailman or something equally as ludicrous?"

"Marnie McCallum was well…" Alice's voice trailed off. She seemed lost in reflection. "I often felt sorry for her. Angus was a drunk and she couldn't help how men chased after her. She was a very nervous, scared woman but so beautiful. I thought Angus abused her too, although no one knew for sure, just like we can't be positive he hit Jake. There's no excuse for Marnie leaving Jake behind when she left. We should have investigated more, but so many people said we should mind our own business. Neither Jake nor Angus appreciated any help."

"Mom, did you keep any of our horses?" Sophie wanted to start riding again.

She hated to see her mother feeling so guilty. Her mother believed she could help and solve everyone's problems. Sophie too felt sorry for Jake. She couldn't imagine what it would feel like to be abandoned by her mother. But there probably wasn't anything Alice could have done to help Marnie or convince her Jake needed her. Marnie had no friends in town. Her melancholy beauty was food for gossip in the tiny community. As was her outlandish shocking behavior. It was rumored she slept with any man in town who asked her.

"No. I only have the house and yard now." Alice sighed. "I'm not sure for how long. Tracy told me she hates that old house on the Dawson property. It's more like a shed and she's right. She asked me to consider moving out of this house."

"Tracy asked you that?" Sophie felt irritation build. It did appear Tracy was taking control of Jake's whole life. She needed to have a talk with Tracy. Her mother loved this house, with all the good memories and times here. She didn't like anyone pressuring her mother to move.

"Are you considering it?"

"Not really. I don't want to move out. And there is really no place in town I want, especially that's for sale."

"What does Jake say?"

"He hasn't said anything." Alice looked at Sophie, then smiled. "I don't know if Tracy is serious and they've discussed it or not. Or she was feeling me out? I doubt I'll move so long as I'm able to look after myself."

"That's the spirit mom. I'd talk to Jake if I were you." Sophie yawned. She was exhausted. "Tracy often saw things differently than others. I mean she always acted so suspicious if any of us even said good morning. She didn't have any friends because she wouldn't let anyone be a friend."

"Well, she's changed. She dresses like she's a housewife with patterned dresses. She removed all those gaudy rings from her face and doesn't dye her hair so black. And she is an excellent cook, so she found her niche and grew up. Everyone wants her baking goods whenever we have our bake sales for the hockey team."

"So the way to a man's heart is through his stomach?" Sophie stretched. Obviously Jake liked to eat, for she could not see any other redeeming qualities about Tracy that he might like. But perhaps she should see the *new* Tracy before she judged. "I'm going to go to bed. I'm exhausted. I still don't know how to cook mom. We mainly had no time and so much take-out while we worked."

"I'll cook you some proper meals. I'm amazed you're still so healthy after eating all that garbage. I can teach you while you're deciding what to do." Alice got up to lock the door and turn the lights out.

Sophie went into the hall again to climb the squeaky, hardwood stairs to the upper floor and bedrooms.

Chapter Four

Sophie could hear the muted sounds of her mother working in the kitchen. The air coming into through the window was cool and refreshing. She pushed back the ruffled bedspread, purple of course, and went to look outside. Various shades of purple were still her favorite color. In the spring lilac bushes outside her bedroom window perpetuated the feelings Sophie loved, connecting to violet. She forgot how much she'd missed it.

Violet curtains fluttered inside the room. The wind was brisk, but not hard. The sky was blue with no clouds in sight. It would be another hot day. But the morning was perfect for riding. It was still cool from the evening mountain air. Sophie loved the wind and realized that was why she wanted to ride again. It had always cleared her head. Hopefully a gallop would help her decide what to do with her life.

Nothing was changed in her room and she felt like a teen instead of the thirty she was. Pictures of celebrities and Randy were glued to her rounded vanity mirror. It was certainly time to redecorate.

Sophie sat down to her mother's breakfast of ham with eggs and homemade bread. "Oh yummy. Haven't had that in ages. Even the bakeries don't make it like you do mom."

Alice laughed. "It is good to have you home Sophie."

"I think I'll go ask Jake for a horse to ride. Unless you want me to do something." She continued, reaching for another piece of bread.

"Sophie, don't go causing trouble please?" Her mother turned from the sink where she was washing dishes. Her hands were beet-red, but that didn't stop Alice from believing dishwashers just didn't get the dishes clean enough. "I think that poor man had enough trouble in his life without you tying him up in knots."

"Mom, I'm fine with Jake marrying Tracy. If that makes him happy I wish them all the best." Inside she wondered how much Tracy had changed. The Tracy she remembered wouldn't make anyone happy. Maybe she would be doing Jake a favor... Quickly she squelched her thoughts. "We can be friends though, can't we?"

"Yes." Alice moved over with a cup of coffee. "I'm glad you're back Sophie. It's so good to have you here for a bit. I take it you slept well and aren't brooding about Dennis?"

"I slept well and no, I'm not even a little upset about Dennis. What he did kind of put my world into a spin, but it's for the best. I was having strong doubts anyway. I feel so much better already."

Her mom reached across to grab Sophie's hand in a tight clasp. "Sophie, maybe it's time to just be on your own for a while. Just don't search for a man to hang onto. Maybe it's time to figure things out without following someone else's opinion."

"I know you're right. It's just that-" Sophie looked up and smiled wistfully. "I've been thinking I would like a baby. I love kids and-"

"Well, it might be best to have a husband first." Alice's tone was matter-of-fact reality when she interrupted. "It's not easy raising children without a father handy."

Sophie nodded, understanding what her mother was saying. She always had a boyfriend and the current boyfriend mainly made her decisions. In high school it was Randy. Everything revolved around Randy and playing hockey. Then after high school in college it was a number of guys, but nothing changed. From Roger, who wanted to be a writer and frequented coffee-shops, Dave who was a musician attending folk festivals to Danny who was interested only in partying and having fun, she realized all the men in her life made her decisions. It was time to make her own choices. But that wouldn't help her have a baby.

It was only about a half mile to the old Dawson place if she cut across the pasture. The air was still cool enough. She wandered among the weeds and wild-flowers. The meadow was covered with swaying grasses as the breeze continued to blow gently. It was a perfect day. Sophie couldn't believe the freedom and lightness she had inside, knowing she didn't have to go into the office, drive with Dennis in heavy traffic or fight crowds of people just to get a good cup of Timmy's coffee. It was exhilarating and she wondered just what she could do here in Crystal Ridge to make a living.

Maybe she could take back her mom's land and run a ranch? She discarded that thought immediately. She had no idea how long Jake's lease was, or how important it was he had their land either. And after ten years without any involvement, and as a teen just helping her dad with ranching, she really didn't know how to run a ranch. Especially the financial aspect might be a challenge she realized. That was one idea she thought she could do and then immediately discarded. What else could she do?

. . .

Sunlight filtered through the clump of trees beside the barn. The forested foothills loomed dark and mysterious in the distance. Jake didn't see the beauty. He was in a foul mood as he yanked the cinch of his saddle. Ally, his chestnut mare shied sideways, giving him a look of reproach. He patted her rump in apology.

Last night Tracy had come over very late, to tell him she would make him a dinner he wouldn't forget tonight. Her questions, subtle but obvious made him wonder - did rumors really circulate that fast? Did Tracy know he gave Sophie a ride from Calgary?

"I hear Sophie Donnelly is back. I heard you drove her home." Tracy confirmed his suspicion.

Instead of listening, he tried to wrack his brains, wondering who'd seen them drive through the Main Street. He admitted he was so busy looking at Sophie he hadn't noticed.

"How did you meet Sophie?" Tracy's words caught his attention.

"Did you tell Alice we were engaged?" Jake counter-acted, wanting to say it was none of her business. She didn't own him – yet. He grimaced. Was this part of marriage? Uncertainties that he was interested in someone else? Orders not to help others?

"No, I did not." Tracy's voice rose sharply. "I think I may have said something about *if we get married*—that's all."

Jake was speechless. He couldn't say who said what. It was rumors. Those rumors that floated around small towns. Everyone knew everyone else's business. And what they didn't know often became a fact by what they assumed.

Yes, he certainly had driven Sophie home. He had kissed her too. He was angry with himself and with Tracy. He remembered Sophie Donnelly. Even back in high-school she had every horny teenage boy on his knees. She was good-natured, always laughing and so gorgeous. He was guilty of watching her often too before he caught himself. Sophie was just a kid and there were more important priorities in his life than chasing after a high-school girl. Sometimes his longings made him feel like a pervert. Especially the day she'd asked him to kiss her. He still didn't know how he'd managed to avoid that. Because that was exactly what he wanted to do, kiss Sophie. But now Sophie was a woman. And she hadn't changed, not even her personality.

Annoyed with his maudlin thoughts, he knew she was just like his mother. High maintenance from the tip of her manicured toenails right to her stylish haircut. Sophie needed attention and it was obvious. Attractive women were a problem he didn't need. He'd spent enough time in chaos and the shadow of a disloyal beautiful woman. He definitely wanted a loyal, good wife. A wife who would help him not cause him unnecessary grief and time. There was no one now to get angry or beat himself up for other people's failings. The reminder should stay forever etched in his mind. He was his own boss. When it came to women and his wife he would summon those memories and make a wise choice.

He just didn't want or need the passionate upheavals that came with beauty. He tried to understand why his mother left his dad. Angus was a surly, gruff man even when he wasn't drinking. But when he was intoxicated, Jake recalled the times Angus hit Marnie just as often as the times he hit his son. Then he felt sorry for his striking mother and hated Angus. That was until she left without a word. Jake eventually learned to avoid Angus and his fits of rage. He spent all his time with Butch learning how to ranch. He couldn't just leave Angus wallowing in his own vomit though. So he went, to make sure Angus hadn't killed himself or to feed and change him.

Jake hated the smell of filth as well. Sophie, like his mother, probably didn't even know how to sweep a floor. He tried to understand his mother's method of avoiding Angus which was to run away with another man. He couldn't blame her for that. But he could blame her for leaving him behind. And he did, even now.

His mother, regardless of how her husband treated her, had no right to leave a twelve-year old boy, defenseless and scared, with Angus. He thought of Dennis's word 'fickle' and nearly chuckled. Sophie found it humorous, but maybe it was a good word to describe both her and his mother.

Tracy, although not beautiful, was a loyal partner, good cook and kept her apartment spotless. She wasn't about to take off and flirt with any guy who paid her attention either. He enjoyed her blunt sarcasm although it kept many men from her. Tracy was perfect for what he needed. Why couldn't he feel happier about that fact?

He hoped thinking of his mother would again bring him back to the ground. Even though Sophie was here in town didn't mean that would change.

He was about to mount when he heard the sound of footsteps on the dusty, dry ground.

There she was. The reason he could falter and not do what he should. Sophie Donnelly, smiling brightly and looking happy to see him again, was irresistible. For a moment he felt like a beam of sunshine surrounded him. He couldn't resist smiling back. His eyes roamed freely over her body, appreciating the fact she'd filled out perfectly in all the right places.

He imagined she probably thought she embodied country. From her tight designer jeans that showed off her long legs, her tight tank top that showed off the fact she didn't need a bra, to her carefully styled modern haircut, she was nothing even close to country. Golden hooped ear-rings dangled almost to her shoulders. She was wearing sandals again.

Realizing he was still smiling like a fool, he sobered. What was she doing? The last thing he wanted was a friendly Sophie. She was much too gorgeous for his taste. Getting involved with Sophie meant a short, volatile relationship until she found someone better. Then painful abandonment when that something better came along. The feeling of desertion he knew well was not worth the risk. The emptiness, the worthlessness and the realization he wasn't loved were all something he was determined to never experience again.

Still, even knowing, he resisted the urge to grab and kiss her. He scowled at his weakness and turned back to his gear.

"What are you doing here?"

"My mom said you might have a horse I could ride." Sophie's voice was light and pleasant.

"Your mom told you that?" Jake scowled in earnest now. He turned to look deliberately at her feet. "In sandals?"   Surely even beautiful women knew they needed boots to ride a horse? Sophie was a rancher's daughter. Shaking his head he turned back to slipping the bridle over Ally's head.

From the looks of Alice last night she seemed determined to keep Sophie under lock and key when he was around. Then he sighed. "I'm going out to get some work done. But you're welcome to any horse in the barn. Where are you going?"

. . .

It was rarely she could keep cross. Life was too short. Jake hadn't done anything wrong except maybe he shouldn't have kissed her. But it was only a comfort kiss, nothing more. And that told her Jake cared when someone was hurting.

"Just out for a ride before it gets too hot."

Jake didn't seem very happy to see her. She threw him a questioning look, wondering what she had done. "Don't worry about me. I rode horses all my life."

Well, it was nearly the truth. For the last ten years she was fortunate if she'd been on a horse a half a dozen times. But it was like riding a bicycle, not something you ever forgot.

Jake led her to the barn. He was silent. Now he reminded her of the Jake she remembered – dark, moody and definitely mysterious. But with his magnificent build, he surely didn't look the same.

"Pick one out. Do you know how to saddle up? I need to get to work."

"My, someone got up on the wrong side of the bed." Sophie gave him a wide-eyed grin. Obviously Jake wasn't a morning person.

He shrugged his shoulders and walked out of the cool, shaded barn.

She picked out Sage, an appaloosa who looked eager to run. He was a grey horse with a spattering of white spots on his rump. She saddled him easily enough. She was thinking that something was wrong with Jake. It was as though he didn't want to see her and it was puzzling. She knew he was engaged to Tracy and she had no intention of horning in on his life. Surely they could be friends, considering he rented her mother's land?

When she got Sage out of the barn and mounted, the horse started bucking instead of running. She didn't have time to think. She felt herself sliding down. It all felt slow-motion, terrifying. Her bottom hit the sod like a brick. Pain shot throughout. Standing, she rubbed the tender spot, now throbbing. She couldn't recall a horse bucking her off since she first started learning to ride.

"Thought you could ride." She looked up and her eyes dropped to the ground. Her whole being flooded with mortification. Jake was still there. Jake saw her.

"Thought you'd gone to work." Sophie mumbled, standing to grab Sage's reins.

Then Jake was off the horse, rubbing his hands down her sides and legs. He was so close she could smell him. Leather and clean crisp air assaulted her. Her eyes fluttered. She was unsure whether it was his touch or the fall making her feel so weak.

"Going to try again?" Was he laughing at her? She heard the underlying humor in his tone.

What was he talking about? Her eyes flew open. *The kiss*? She chose to think it was riding the horse.

"Is this another of your horses you lend to the rodeo for the bucking bronco events?" Sophie felt her eyes sparking as disappointment invaded. He wouldn't be so cruel. But she didn't know Jake or anything about him.

"No, Sophie he's not." Jake's touch moved up to hold her arms to her side. His eyes were soothing and filled with concern. Sophie still felt embarrassment flooding throughout. He didn't look at all mean. His eyes were filled with genuine anxiety. "Are you alright? No broken bones?"

His hands moved again swiftly down her arms, to her sides and he bent to touch her hips and waist. Sophie felt no discomfiture. It was the opposite. His hand were simultaneously hot yet consoling. She felt the desire licking through her veins. Teetering, she nearly fell against him. Jake took that moment to look into her eyes. His eyes were potent, as though trying to draw her right into himself. She was falling. Only this time it was delightful. Willingly, she plunged into the promise of paradise she could see, she could feel.

"I'm fine…" Her words were lost, enveloped by his kiss again. Aggressive, yet gentle this wasn't a kiss of comfort. Desire ran rampant. It was a kiss of need, a kiss of wanting more…

"Damn!" Jake stepped back first. He was breathing heavily and he wouldn't look at her. "We can't have a relationship Sophie. I don't want a relationship…"

"With me." Sophie finished his sentence. She sank to the ground in humiliation. "You're engaged to Tracy."

"Well, not exactly engaged, but I'm considering it. Tracy is right for me. You're not." Jake turned to grab Ally's reins. It was amazing how much his words hurt.

He was right. She had no business coming back to break up his life. She looked up. "Jake, I don't want a relationship with you. I just want us to be friends. Stop kissing me though…please?" Her voice was weak and held no conviction.

"You're right, it's my fault, not yours." Jake flushed, looking away. "Come tomorrow and I'll ride with you. Don't go riding today. I'm late and really have to get out and help the boys today. Make sure to come early enough I can get out working at a decent time." He mounted and kicked Ally into motion without looking at Sophie.

Sophie felt the urge to defy him, but realized he was right - lying somewhere in the wilderness with broken bones wouldn't be very pleasant. She turned to lead Sage back into the barn.

Sophie's disgrace increased when her heart had leapt up in response to his words. A ride with Jake was certainly a pleasant idea, way too pleasant. And now she knew Tracy had lied to her mother. Jake and Tracy were not engaged. She was anything but proud of her thoughts.

    Determined to be strong, she tilted her chin. She would not interfere with his plans. She would even attempt to befriend Tracy again. Maybe her mother was right and Tracy was changed. People did grow up and adjust. She couldn't judge Tracy by her high-school behavior.

Chapter Five

After her disastrous attempt at riding, Sophie went home and asked her mother if she could borrow her pick-up and go into town. Sputtering and protesting she finally got the old rusted vehicle out of the yard. It was obvious her mother needed a new vehicle. On the narrow, two lane and familiar highway that led into town, worry once again plagued her mind. What could she do? She couldn't just play at being a kid again. She wanted to work. She needed to do something.

She stuck her folded arm out the open window and the air rushed through, pushing her worries aside. She turned the radio up, singing along with the blaring song. It was an effective way for Sophie to block problems out. A fast vehicle and the radio helped. Then she giggled, wondering how fast she could go in her mother's old Ford. Would it stay together? Today the quartz mountain reflected like diamonds in the morning sun. Pines and brush grew, tangled and twisted, from the steep side. She felt nostalgia creep in, nostalgia for those days when she rode beside the beautiful cliff.

She looked out over the fields, resisting the temptation to try speeding in her mother's truck. Here by the road, grass filled the ditches and sagging barbed-wire fences kept the herds of cattle from roaming up on the highway. Towering hills and tall pines created a shadow on the road, blocking it from the bright sun.

Main Street was little changed, a long wide corridor with angle parking. From the small jewelry store, an electronic repair store to Christine's dress shop on a corner, even the cracks in the sidewalk seemed the same. Further down the road she could see the yellow grocery store building. When she had lived here, the store seemed so big. Now she realized it wasn't much bigger than some of the convenience stores in Calgary. It all looked just as it had ten years ago.

Turning the corner, she noticed something changed. There was a small section of Pine Street with covered board-walks. A few shops here were log-faced, creating a western theme. There was a gift shop, a book store and a café. Cowboy Coffee caught her eye, so she pulled into a parking spot. She recalled visiting the cafe those times she didn't need to catch a school bus to go home. Randy had his own truck and her parents weren't so strict they wouldn't let her join in with the others after school. They said she should enjoy this time and they were right. Could anyone capture the carefree time, being a teenager?

Inside the softly lit interior she noticed the small tables with wooden chairs weren't much different from when Isabelle and Carl Cruise ran the only café in town. Ryan, their son and another classmate, was standing, polishing a counter. He looked up in surprise as the door jingled.

"Sophie, as I live and breathe…" He came from around the counter and enveloped her in a big hug. Tall and thin with auburn hair and blue eyes that twinkled, Ryan hadn't changed much.

"I don't think I've seen you since high-school" Sophie hugged him back. Ryan was one of their group and of course a hockey player. "Where are your parents?"

"They retired and moved to Arizona. This is their legacy to me," Ryan laughed, letting her go. "Not much, but better than nothing."

"I noticed you made a few changes."

The windows were covered in slated, wooden blinds instead of the gingham frilly curtains Isabelle insisted on. And there were no more potted dried floral plants on the tables or arrangements hanging on the walls. It looked more rustic with black and white pictures of rodeo events and a set of large horns adorning the wall over the door.

Sophie climbed up on a tall stool by the granite counter. "Can I have a coffee? I hope you've kept that the same. Your mom sure knew how to make coffee."

"That she did. So I kept it the same." Grinning, Ryan went behind the counter and grabbed a mug. He reached for a coffee-pot and poured her some. "Cream and sugar?"

"Just black." Sophie wrapped her hands around the mug and studied the bubbles.

"What are you doing back in Crystal Ridge? Are you visiting your mom? How are Dennis, Pat and Bill? I hear you guys are corporate big-shots or something now." Ryan kept polishing the glasses lined up behind the counter.

"Or something for sure." Sophie grimaced and looked up at Ryan. "I just broke up with Dennis and came back to make a few decisions."

"Sorry to hear that. But really you and Randy were much better suited than you and our local math genius. You're not heartbroken are you?"

"More my pride" Sophie explained with no emotion. No she was definitely not heartbroken. In fact, she was moving on very fast and didn't like where it was heading at all. Jake belonged to another, yet she wanted him. She didn't say any of that to Ryan. "And you?"

"Molly and I are married. We are just waiting for our second kid."

"Two babies? Congratulations" Sophie sounded envious because she was. It was no joke, she really wanted a baby. That much she knew. It was getting a husband and a job that was baffling her now. Guys didn't seem so willing to marry pretty girls, just use them, she thought bitterly and made an effort to cheer up.

Molly was having her second baby.

Molly and Ryan were both in her class at school. They dated throughout high school and married shortly after. Molly was often part of Sophie's and Pat's activities when she wasn't with Ryan.

"Are you going to just leave your share of the business?" Ryan asked after pouring her another coffee. He came around the counter and he hopped up on a stool beside her. He took her hands in his.

"I see you're still antsy Ryan. Can't sit still?"

Ryan threw her a wry grin, but stayed silent.

His question brought Sophie back to her problem. "I don't know for sure. I don't know much about the business, just worked there. Dennis did all the finance part. Maybe I can sell my portion and have some money." That just made her ask more questions. What would she do with the money? Maybe there was none and Dennis had just put it all back into the company. But then wouldn't that make her portion of the company worth something?

"You took web-design courses I heard." Ryan continued. "Why don't you start your own business here – an online business? You could stay in Crystal Ridge and work from home. I remember you always loved the country."

"Well it was a toss-up. Randy or my horse." Sophie didn't know if she wanted to start a business from scratch. Would starting a new company take up too much of her time again? And without accounting experience, how could she run it alone? When would she have time to marry and have a baby? She was too confused to make plans for her future. For nearly ten years all her plans involved the business and Dennis.

"Well, both Molly and I know a little about finances." Ryan interrupted her thoughts. "If you need help just ask. And I hear Jake is pretty good with that as well. I guess you know he's leasing your mom's land eh? You don't need Dennis the math genius."

"Thanks for the offer. Why do you keep calling Dennis the math genius?"

"Cause that's what he is and he always let everyone know."

But Sophie was thinking about Jake again. "Do you know Jake that well?"

"Yes. He and Tracy come over to the house often. Sometimes we go out to the bar together for a break. Molly appreciates that. She's pretty busy."

"I bet. What's your child's name? I'll have to stop in and see her." Were Molly and Tracy good friends? Like everyone else Tracy hadn't been very nice to Molly either. She must have changed. Apparently everyone in town liked Tracy now.

"It's Emma. And Molly would love to see you again. Can you take some of your clients from Dennis or are they tied in with the company?" Ryan immediately reverted back to questions about the company. And her mother said she couldn't hold a thought?

"Ryan, I really don't know." Sophie felt guilty. She had left her friends and even Dennis in an awkward position. Technical support and web-design were what the company was all about. And she handled the web-design part. Now Ryan was asking about stealing clients. Was it unethical?

"Well," He bounced back up and went around the counter. Ryan lowered his eyes to polish a glass. "How about you work here until you figure it out. Not much – a little cooking, a little cleaning and a little waitressing. Sometimes I want to go with Molly, especially for her appointments but don't often have the chance if Trudy is off."

"Ryan, I don't know how to cook." Sophie admitted. Leaning over the counter she whispered loudly, "I hear that's a tragedy and may well be the reason I can't keep a man."

"Your mom tell you that?" Ryan sputtered. "It sounds like Alice."

He poured her more coffee. "I'll teach you how to cook. Molly isn't much of a cook either. Maybe I'm the fool, marrying her. I didn't realize I should marry a woman who cooks."

The door jingled again. Ryan looked up. Sophie swirled sideways on her rotating stool to see who was coming in. A little boy about ten years old with a scowl on his face, came to the counter.

"Come to see if you can give me a few hours of work Ryan." The little boy climbed up on a stool. His attitude was very defensive. A lost, confused boy attempting to be strong was visible in his jutting jaw but sad eyes. "I just can't seem to gather up enough money for my hockey this year."

"Aren't you supposed to be in school buddy?" Ryan grinned, shrugging his shoulders at Sophie's inquiring look.

"Naw,' remember its summer? Mom's feeling sickly again. I stuck around to help her or Ida been in this morning." The boy's voice was casual, but listening carefully, they both could hear the underlying fear in his voice.

"Is she alright now? You want a snack before I get you to sweep the floor?" Ryan cut a huge piece of pie. Placing a dollop of ice-cream over it and pouring a large glass of milk, he placed it before the boy.

"Sophie, this is Dominic Reynolds. He and his parents live in Angus McCallum's old place on Cedar Street." Ryan supplied nonchalantly, his eyes begging Sophie not to say anything. "Along with his three brothers and sisters. His dad is a mechanic. Your dad working yet Dominic?"

Sophie remained silent, studying Dominic. The poor boy. That shack had four rooms and she couldn't imagine how six people could live there.

"No. Damn garage fired him, just 'cause he was sick and took a day off." Dominic was obviously repeating his father's words. He dug right into the pie, almost exhuming it in one gulp.

So much left unsaid, so much revealed. Sophie wished she could help this little boy. "How old are you Dominic?"

"I'm nearly ten already," Dominic looked up from his pie. His blue eyes widened. "You sure are pretty ma'am."

Sophie smiled. Dominic's compliment was sincere and didn't make her feel awkward at all.

The door jingled again. Bowing her head quickly, Sophie peeked up at Tracy. Or at least she thought it must be Tracy. Her hair was no longer black, her clothes were no longer black and she had no rings on her still pale, plain face. Tracy sat at a table by the window, ignoring Sophie.

"Hey, Dominic you want to take Tracy a glass of water before you start sweeping?" Ryan suggested. "You just want coffee Tracy?"

Tracy nodded, turning to look at Sophie. She still made no effort to acknowledge her. Did she recognize her?

It was soon obvious Ryan's suggestion was a mistake. Dominic hopped off the chair, grabbing the water glass Ryan put on the counter. He walked slowly over to Tracy's table, holding the glass carefully. Then he tripped on his untied shoelace. All hell broke loose. Tracy shrieked as she stood up, dripping water.

"You pathetic little brat, you did that deliberately." Tracy yelped, her usual pale face turning red. "Ryan, why on earth do you humor this *horrible* boy?"

Ryan rushed around the counter with a cloth to help dry Tracy's brown suit jacket and pencil skirt. Without realizing what she was doing Sophie got up and took Dominic's arm. She wanted to hug him. He looked terrified. "Come Dominic, you can get me more coffee, please?"

"Get off me you creep!" Tracy pushed Ryan away. Her face twisted with fury and hatred as she turned to Sophie. "I see the bitch queen is back. Nothing has changed. You always cause chaos. You asked him to do that for a laugh, didn't you?"

Startled, Sophie's mouth dropped open. What on earth did Tracy's ramblings mean? Was Tracy blaming Sophie for causing this scene?

Ignoring Tracy's ludicrous accusation, Sophie walked around the counter and reached for the coffee pot. She handed it to Dominic, and let him pour coffee into her cup. His hands trembled, but he concentrated by twisting his tongue, careful not to spill it.

Sophie looked at Ryan, standing helpless with a cloth dangling from his fingers. Tracy, still fuming, glared at Sophie as she walked towards the door.

"Child labor is illegal and there's a reason why Ryan. Children are incompetent." She went stomping out.

"Oh my." Sophie couldn't think of what to say. Her mother said Tracy was different? Well, her exterior looked different and with insight Sophie realized her nature might be too, but only around specific others. Sophie didn't appear to be one of them. "You said she had changed?"

"No, I didn't say that. I said she and Jake came over to the house. She is nice when Jake's around and she's trying to impress him." Ryan stopped as though realizing he shouldn't be talking. Dominic, close by, could hear.

Right now Sophie worried about how Dominic was feeling, not Tracy. Ryan brought him a mop. She noticed Dominic went to clean up any water spots around the table Tracy had sat first. His shoulders trembled and he kept his eyes glued to the floor.

It was obvious Tracy didn't care for kids. Children could be conscientious. Dominic was one of them.

"So what's the story?" Sophie asked, still watching Dominic and wanting to go help him. He was only ten. He didn't deserve Tracy's treatment.

Ryan climbed on the stool beside her.

"I'm sorry Tracy yelled at you. She's nice when she and Jake come in the restaurant."

"Of course she is," Sophie nodded understanding what Ryan insinuated. Tracy wanted to fool the town into thinking she was wonderful so she would be able to trap Jake. "But I'm more worried how Dominic is feeling. Is there something I can do to help?"

"His father is a useless drunk. And it looks like Jim beats the kids and Dominic's mom, Millie. Dominic said she was sick, but I think Jim hit her. Unless Millie presses charges or leaves him, I can't do much. Dominic doesn't tell me what's going on either. He's the oldest and Millie has a baby. So I bet he has to stay home to care for the kids when Jim hits Millie."

"Why is Dominic working here?" Sophie pressed on, puzzled. Shouldn't Ryan insist on Dominic going to school or helping his mother?

"Dominic is a good little hockey player and he wants to play so much. They don't have enough money for him to play. I want to give him the chance but as you notice he's a proud little thing. So I give him work and he feels he is earning it."

"What a nice thing to do," Sophie put her hand on Ryan's shoulder and squeezed. "I want to help too. Why do little ones have problems? It's so unfair. What can I do?"

"Maybe you could take him into Calgary to get his equipment before the fall. You can use the money I give you and he thinks he's worked for it. With Molly pregnant and me working here so much, it's hard to get into the city."

"I have money too Ryan. Let's split the cost and get Dominic into hockey. I can't wait to go to his games. I always loved hockey."

"Oh yeah, Sophie prom queen and Randy hockey star – the town's golden couple." There was no resentment in Ryan's tone.

"More like bitch queen I hear," Sophie corrected him. She felt sadness invade. Poor Jake. If he married Tracy he might learn to regret it. She may look different, but Tracy's personality hadn't changed whatsoever. She had just learned how to hide it. "Mom said Tracy is a great cook and I hope that's enough for Jake."

"She has most the town duped over her change." Ryan shook his head. "She even had me wondering. But I guess she can't hide her dislike for children. Come to think of it, she never asks to hold Emma. She ignores her."

"Did you see Dominic's face? He looks devastated. Better give him some praise." Sophie walked over to the door. Her mom was meeting with her friends at the church tonight and needed her vehicle. "I want to go riding in the morning. I'll come in again after my ride. You can teach me how to cook. Bye Dominic! Will you be here tomorrow?"

"Bye Sophie." Dominic looked up and smiled sweetly. "I try and come in every day in the summer. I'll teach you how to cook too. I know some. You don't know how to cook. But you're a girl."

"That sounds fun." Sophie was laughing. "Beware, not all girls know how to cook.

"Okay," Ryan was laughing too and walked through the swinging doors into the kitchen. "My specialty is my Eggs Benedict and we'll start with that."

"I sure hope you're joking," Sophie felt anxious, laughter forgotten. *'Eggs Benedict'*. Even the name sounded ominous.

Chapter Six

Jake was at the barn with two saddled horses the following morning. The sun was bright but the morning air was still cool. He had a scowl on his face that didn't encourage conversation. Was Jake still a moody, complex man? Or did he hate getting out of bed?

"Betsy." He grunted, handing her the reins. Betsy looked like an old, fat farm horse. Her eyes were drooping and watery. Her hair was mousy and laced with grey. Sophie wanted to laugh. Betsy was nothing like Sage. Instead she mounted without commenting and followed Jake's lead.

She found Jake's trail easy to follow. He moved onto the Donnelly land and she was sure she knew every nook and cranny the land offered. All her memories came back and she was happy to be silent as well. Betsy could run, just not as fast as she might like. It was going to be baby steps with Jake.

"Jake, do you know Dominic Reynolds?" She broke the silence and urged Betsy to move beside Jake's stallion.

"The kid in dad's old house? Yeah, the family are distant cousins of mine. Jim came to look after dad after I moved out. Dominic is the oldest." Jake answered non-committal and short.

Sophie's breath caught in her throat. It was more like Millie, the one who had looked after Angus. Jim sounded just like Angus. Did the two men sit and drink together? Did Jim abuse Dominic now, like Angus supposedly abused Jake? Did she dare ask Jake?

"Jake, did Angus hit you? Does Jim hit Dominic?" She wanted to shut her mouth but the words poured out. Jake's eyes were cold and hard when he looked at her. He said nothing.

Why did these things happen and why was there nothing that could be done about it? Jake's silence and resentment spoke volumes.

"Dominic said he's ten. He's still a baby. We can't just let..." Sophie continued. Jake wasn't responsive. Once long ago people said Jake played good hockey too, until he couldn't afford to play. So it was logical to assume he and Dominic had a lot in common. "He wants so badly to play hockey."

"That kid that will do anything to play hockey. I know that." Was there a wistful tone in Jake's casual voice?

"The kid *is* going to play hockey." Sophie stated. "Ryan is helping him and I'm going to as well."

"Sophie," Jake turned to look at her shaking his head. "There are times you have to mind your own business, like it or not. You can get hurt getting involved."

"I won't be hurt like he is." Sophie felt tears welling in her eyes, blurring the countryside. She blinked. "I would have the police there so fast. And I would make sure my charges stayed."

"Then what?" Jake's eyes were still hard when he looked at her. "Jim goes to jail for a bit. Then he gets out and matters are worse. If anything is going to happen Millie has to leave him. And what is she going to do with four kids? Besides, even with a restraining order, Jim won't stay away. She won't be safe either way. Bastards like him should be killed. But I'm not going to jail for scum like him."

"Ryan said-"

"Ryan is married, Sophie. Tracy said you were there yesterday flirting with him," Jake sounded mad.

"Flirting with him?" Sophie knew Tracy hadn't changed. Tracy was a liar. "Molly and I were always good friends. I have no intentions of trying to get Ryan. He's my friend."

Sophie was indignant. But Jake would believe what he wanted. There was no point arguing with him. "Regardless, Ryan and I... and Molly I'm sure, are going to make sure Dominic can play hockey. He is such a proud little boy. He wants to work for his money. I just wondered if you had any suggestions."

"Because I wanted the same thing when I was his age? Because I could never figure out how to get the money? Why would I know how to now?" Jake's eyes were defensive and filled with pain when he turned to her.

"Forget I even mentioned it." Sophie winced, trying to kick Betsy into a gallop.

Was it possible Jake was like Tracy and hated kids too? It didn't matter. His whole attitude was something she didn't want to recognize he possessed. It was the first time she'd seen Jake angry and sullen. She didn't like it at all. If she kept this moment foremost in her mind, she would be able to forget how attractive he was.

"I'm sorry. That remark wasn't necessary. It's a good thing what you are trying to do. I was like him and I didn't want the town's charity either. It always came with a price I didn't want to pay." Jake kept his horse beside hers. She knew she couldn't outrun his horse. "You're bringing back memories I want to forget Sophie."

"What's the price you pay for charity?" Sophie was curious and just as her uneasiness surfaced, it dissipated. This was the Jake she was falling in love with. Now, angry with herself, she blocked out that train of thought.

"Some people want to help." Jake continued, sounding sad and hesitant. "But there are some that expect you will feed their ego and be forever grateful for the crumbs they give you. It was as though I was their ticket into heaven or something. As a kid, I didn't know the difference, so I just didn't take help from anyone."

"That makes sense." Sophie wanted to comfort him, but didn't dare. She was well aware of what happened whenever she touched Jake. "How can I help Dominic, without him believing I want him to be my ticket into heaven?"

"I'm not sure. People like me and Dominic are hard to get through. When I hit the teen years I didn't want charity of any kind. I would help you now, but I'm kind of busy. A ranch can't run itself." Jake slanted her a slow grin. "I'm taking more time away from work than I should as it is."

Sophie flushed. Yes, just by riding with her, he was interfering with his work. She wanted to convince him she was able to ride on her own, especially with Betsy. She knew well how valuable time was for a rancher.

"Ryan is giving him money to help in the café. He asked if I would take Dominic into town and get him some hockey equipment. I agreed."

"I would suggest you let Dominic pay for his equipment and let the sales clerk realise you'll cover the difference. That will save Dominic's pride."

"I already figured that out." Sophie nodded, smiling. She wanted to tell him about the incident with Tracy in the café but didn't. Jake wanted to marry Tracy just the way she was. Perhaps they both didn't want children.

"Jake, do you and Tracy want children?" She asked instead of ignoring her idea not to say anything. Well, information like that was important. And if he said he didn't, she would do everything in her power to stop liking this man.

"W-what?" Jake stuttered, looking at her. "Sophie, Tracy and I haven't even discussed marriage yet, let alone talk about having kids"

"I can help with Dominic in the winter." He changed the subject. "Right now, we're branding the spring calves and we have to move some of the herds into the hills. It's getting too dry."

"I realize how busy you must be at this time of the year." Sophie assured him. "I haven't forgotten what it was like for dad. You don't have to ride with me. I'm not sure what happened yesterday. I guess Sage caught me by surprise."

"You shouldn't wear sandals when you're riding."

"I can't find my boots and I haven't got any new ones."

He laughed at her flimsy excuse. "When you take Dominic to Calgary, you'll have to get yourself a pair of boots."

She drove into town after. Today she would learn how to make Eggs Benedict. And from the scorched, sometimes burnt sauces it was as difficult as she imagined. Eventually she managed to make a light fluffy sauce, not lumpy, not burnt. It was all in the heat of the pan and how you whisked it, Ryan advised. Finally she developed the patience to make it slow and careful.

The coffee-shop was busy for the whole afternoon, Sophie agreed to stay and help him. Ryan had to cook but she poured coffee and brought plates of food to the table at least.

She realized she'd stayed too long when Tracy and Jake came in for supper. It was painful to see the two together. Carefully she kept her smile in place, that phony smile she had perfected over the years. The smile that hid all her thoughts. She tried to ignore the flutter in her stomach, seeing Jake.

"Hello Sophie. It's been a long time." Tracy gushed, coming to give her a hug. "Are you going to work here? Aren't you part owner of a big-shot computer company in Calgary?"

Nearly, Sophie's jaw dropped. But she kept her smile in place. Talk about phony.

"But you were in here yesterday." Sophie continued to smile as she placed the menus on the table, along with a glass of water. She fought the urge to tip Tracy's glass. She didn't like the way Tracy wasn't being honest with Jake. But she had no way of warning Jake, or even knowing if Jake cared.

"I didn't stay and chat because that silly little boy poured that glass of water on me. Fortunately it wasn't coffee."

"Yes, fortunate for sure. Oh excuse me." Sophie turned to smile at the couple walking into the café. Inside she was angry.

Silly little boy? Didn't Jake realize Tracy didn't like children? Then her heart sank imagining Jake didn't like children either. He never did say whether he did or didn't.

"Jake is taking me out tonight to reward me for the wonderful roast-beef dinner I cooked him last night." Tracy immediately explained when Sophie came back to take their order.

"That's nice." Sophie managed, feeling tongue-tied and awkward. She made herself busy, pouring coffee and not looking at Jake. Jealousy ate inside, more vehemently and ugly than she could imagine.

"I made Yorkshire pudding with it." Tracy's eyes were sparkling, making her angular face almost pretty. "Maybe we can get together and exchange recipes. Jake said it's the best he ever tasted."

"Sure," Sophie continued to smile wondering if she should say *'well, I learned how to make decent Eggs Benedict'*. "What would you like?"

Sophie really didn't cook well at all. In fact after her attempts with the Hollandaise sauce, she wasn't sure if she even wanted to know how to cook. In Calgary, they went out to restaurants with clients or had take-out food. There was no time to cook.

She wondered if something like that was important to Jake. Should she become 'Suzie Homemaker' and would that make Jake like her better? Did men not want to marry her because she lacked culinary skills? She felt Jake's eyes on her and wondered if he could read her mind. She flushed and looked away. His smile was gentle.

He reached over and patted Tracy's hand. "Yes, I'm glad you are a good cook. Otherwise the boys and I would starve to death."

Sophie tried to hide how much his affection towards Tracy hurt. Well, all things considered, wasn't that a shallow reason to marry someone? And people called her shallow?

She went into the kitchen and leaned against the wall, looking at Ryan. "They want your meat-loaf dinner."

"What's wrong Sophie?" Ryan looked up, blowing on his red face. The grill was obviously hot.

"Nothing. Is Molly really friends with Tracy? That woman…"

"…is very irritating?" Ryan laughed. He reached for two plates and began arranging them with ingredients. "No, it's more like Jake and I are friends and lately Tracy tags along. They've only started dating. Seriously I don't have a clue what he sees in her."

"And Molly is polite to her? Has Molly changed so much?"
Sophie recalled Molly, a cute curly haired blonde, outspoken and chipper. Molly knew how to make those single, sarcastic remarks better than anyone Sophie knew. To Sophie they were so funny, but in fairness never directed towards her and just as often directed against Tracy.

"Not much. But her mocking remarks often go over Tracy's head or else Tracy, who is very obviously trying to impress Jake, doesn't respond. I don't think they should get married Do you?"

"How would I know? Jake seems so nice and kind and Tracy hasn't changed." Sophie didn't want to say too much, even to Ryan. "But Tracy does sound nice too - when she's with him."

"I hear you're going riding with him in the mornings."

Sophie laughed, forgetting her concerns. There were no secrets in a small town. "And does that make Jake a player? Is he dating two girls now according to the grape-vine? Mom never kept any horses and I want to ride. Jake's horses are very close by and he said I can ride them."

"But I hear he comes riding with you." Ryan put garnish on the plates.

"What? One day and already Jake comes riding with me?" Sophie sputtered. How could she not remember this aspect of small town living? "Jake and I are just friends Ryan."

Ryan nodded, dropping his eyes to the grill. Sophie reached for the prepared plates and went through the swinging doors again. She noticed Jake was staring out the window and Tracy was busy studying her cutlery. They sure didn't act like two love-birds.

"Thank you." They both murmured as she set the plates down.

"Would you like anything else?"

"A new knife perhaps," Tracy's voice was gentle and sweet. "This has spots on it. Are you washing dishes too Sophie?"

Sophie gasped, not believing her ears. Furious, she recalled the conversation with her mother. It was time to fight back. She just couldn't stay silent, even when she knew she should. Tracy was still a bitch and now Jake could see it too.

"I hear you two are bugging my mom to give up her house. I suggest you leave her alone. She doesn't want to move."

"Bugging your mom..." Jake's eyes were both puzzled and startled when he turned to look at Sophie. He looked at Tracy. A muscle jerked in his jaw as though he was clenching his teeth.

"Well, that Dawson place is no more than a shack." Tracy looked defensive and guilty. "We can't really live there when we get married. I just thought I'd put a bug in her ear and have her consider it."

"When we get married? Alice mentioned that too the other day and I just thought it was a rumor like so many that circulate around town because we've dated. Then you said you didn't say that." Jake sounded utterly confused. He looked up at Sophie and his voice was harsh. "Tracy won't be bugging your mom again. Will you, Tracy?"

But Jake took Tracy's hand and that was all Sophie noticed. His words were an indiscernible buzz in her ears.

"Make sure you don't." Sophie whirled and went back into the kitchen. It sounded like Tracy was at the ranch all the time... cooking. Maybe they were already... she flushed at that thought. Here in Crystal Ridge it might still be important they were married before they just shacked up.

"Hey, cheer up Sophie. It's not like you to look so sad," Ryan came to put his arm around her. "I have an idea. I'll call Molly to see if she could meet us at Big Al's for a drink. She can't drink alcohol of course, but she's excited to see you again and catch up. She can ask Denise next door to babysit."

"Finally," Sophie valiantly pushed her depressing thoughts aside. She could not, she would not fall in love with Jake. "We can go into Big Al's and not be kicked out."

Big Al's was the only bar in town. As teen's, on a dare, they sometimes tried to go into the bar. But being such a small town, of course everyone knew their age. It became a game, a game they always lost. Many conversations centered on that intriguing place.

"I'd love to catch up with Molly." Sophie agreed.

Chapter Seven

Big Al's was crowded and dark. Music was loud and voices were muffled with laughter and hoots. The dance floor was packed. Sophie looked around at the old wagon wheel chandeliers giving little light to the dark room. A long bar ran along one side, a fenced-in small dance area and small wooden tables and chairs finished the interior. It was basic and set up to give customers their drinks. But seeing it for the first time still created a bit of excitement and anticipation.

Ryan placed his hand on her back and guided her into the room. Her heart sank when he went straight to the table Jake and Tracy were seated at. Neither Jake nor Tracy looked happy when they looked up to greet them. Tracy would have looked better wearing her gothic outfit here. Everyone was wearing jeans and shirts or T-shirts. Only Tracy was wearing a light, printed dress. With the lacy peter-pan collar and frilled skirt, she looked country, but more housewife, go to church country. Jake leaned over to whisper in Tracy's ear. Green envy reared its' ugly head again, more vehement than anything she'd experienced watching Dennis kiss Liz. Sophie turned to smile at Ryan trying to ignore them.

Taking their seats Ryan yelled above the noise. "Molly should be here in a few minutes."

Jake looked up to study Sophie. Sophie stared back, feeling like a bug under a scope. What was he looking for? Did he think she didn't want Molly to come? He must have read her mind. He smiled and shook his head. Then he turned back to Tracy. Sophie was reminded of Dennis and Liz. But this time Jake belonged to Tracy, not her and her heart sank. The injury of that awareness was an awful feeling.

With false bravado she looked at Ryan instead. "Dance with me."

It had been so long. Sometimes Bill, Pat's fiancée, would take pity on her and dance. Sometimes, even though she knew Dennis didn't like it, she would accept a stranger's offer to dance. Sophie loved dancing and had never considered it to mean anything but fun, not a flirting activity like some said.

"You know I never dance." Ryan grinned to soften his rejection. "Sorry. But there are loads of guys around you know that would probably fall over themselves if you asked."

"Yes Sophie." Tracy inserted sweetly, indicating she was listening to their conversation. Jake did not look pleased.
"There's Simon over there or AJ sitting with Doris. Remember them – they were in our class too." Tracy continued.

Sophie looked around. Simon was heavy-lidded and rocking on his chair. Oh yes, she remembered. Simon had been into heavy drinking even in high-school. Nothing seemed changed. AJ was seated with Doris and they both looked uptight with stern expressions on their bleary-eyed faces. Tracy would love to see her get involved with their obvious squabble.

She threw Tracy a scornful look, resisting the temptation to make a scathing remark.

"Well Pete looks sober and he's standing at the bar. He was Dennis's friend." Ryan put his hand on her arm squeezing. "He always liked you too."

"All the boys liked Sophie." Jake stood abruptly and reached out his hand. "Come on Sophie, I'll dance with you."

Startled, Sophie took his hand, not daring to look at Tracy. She owed Tracy nothing she thought, squelching her guilt. They moved to the dance floor. Did Jake care she wanted to dance? Was he jealous, thinking she might dance with another man? She tossed her hopes aside. He was only being kind, gentle Jake and taking pity on her because she had no one to dance with.

The first song was a fast two-step. Submersing herself into the music, Sophie was glad to see Jake knew how to dance very well. As he twirled and led her around the floor she could only enjoy the activity, made special by the fact she was dancing with Jake, not a stranger.

But the second song was a slow ballad by George Strait and she knew she would make a fool of herself, dancing so close. It was better for her equilibrium, not being close to Jake.

"Let's sit down," She suggested out of breath as she considered it. And made the mistake of looking into his smoldering eyes.

He pulled her into his arms and whispered softly into her ear. "No my little Sophie. Let's dance."

She melted, unable to resist this potent Jake. She wanted to look back at Tracy but didn't dare. It would surely ruin her moment. Just for a bit, she would enjoy this and pretend... She didn't have to explain, he did. And Jake had broad shoulders. If he didn't care why should she?

Then it was too late. His arms flexed against her side and he was squeezing her hand. She felt him pull her closer until she was against him. It was excruciating, it was beautiful. His hot chest pressed against her bosom, his tensed hips touched against hers as they moved and she wanted to moan. Delight rampaging throughout, she couldn't have stood on her own if she tried.

'When did you stop loving me," Strait was crooning too poignant and truthful. She gave a small gasp, oddly thinking of Dennis when all she wanted was to enjoy this moment. Tears welled in her eyes. No one would love her 'forever'.

"Sophie, what's wrong?" Jake seemed in tune with her thoughts. Both hands reached up to cup her face. He stopped dancing. His thumbs reached to wipe across her eyes gently.

"I don't know Jake." She whispered back. "Hearing this song I thought about Dennis, but I didn't love him. So why do I care.

Or am I so selfish, I want a guy's attention, even though I don't want him?"

"You might have hit it on the head." Jake's lips twisted in a wry smile but he continued stroking her cheeks, wiping the tears away. "Why do you need all those guys chasing you Sophie? Why can't one guy be enough for you?"

"It's unfair to say that Jake. One guy was enough. I dated Dennis for ten years and I was faithful." Sophie shook her head in confusion and started moving. "Come on Jake. People are watching us. So is Tracy. It's obvious you're fighting with her. What about you? Are you trying to make her jealous?"

"Not really. She doesn't own me, but lately she's acting like she does. We've only dated Sophie." He moved his hands and started dancing properly again. He was still holding her much closer than he should be.

"Are you living with her? It sounds like she's always out at the ranch." Sophie stated with accusation in her tone. Then realized she should have stayed silent. It really wasn't her business and she shouldn't talk.

"No, she doesn't live at the ranch. I haven't asked her to marry me. I took her out some and she's a great cook. I don't know what she's thinking, but she's talking like it's a done deal and I don't know how she got that idea. But honestly Sophie, I have considered it." Jake's face looked grim and serious now. He stepped back a bit. "Tracy will make the perfect rancher's wife and I should accept that."

"Yes you should because it doesn't look that way from here." Sophie snapped and then wanted to bite her tongue. It sounded like she cared and she didn't want to give him that impression.

"Do you love her?" Sophie changed the topic, refusing to acknowledge the wounded feelings seeping within.

Jake missed a step, looking down at her with surprise. Then he laughed softly. "Is that a requirement? From everything

I've seen, love doesn't last. Isn't it better to just choose your partner by whether they suit you or not?"

"Jake," Sophie was shocked as she tried to move back. He pulled her closer instead. "Does Tracy know about you not loving her? Talk about callous and you call me selfish?"

"I never called you selfish." Jake stopped her movement by flexing his arms. He sang in her ear. *'There was a time when you worshipped where I stood. Heaven knows I'd bring it back if I could.'* I don't think you're selfish at all. You once generously offered..." Jake had a very nice voice, when he interrupted his comment to sing in her ear.

"Jake," Sophie tried to pull out of his arms. "That was so long ago. I was a kid."

"Ah, so you do remember." Jake wouldn't let her escape. "But I wasn't talking about you. I was talking about me."

Feeling queasy and anxious Sophie remained silent. What was he talking about?

"That's true Sophie. I did worship you. You caused me many guilty moments when I was young and foolish. Let's enjoy the music."

Was it true that he worshipped her or was he just teasing? Why didn't she know? Occasionally she would meet Jake when he was out on the Dawson ranch and she was riding. He was always kind and polite, but never indicated he *worshipped* her. He treated her like she was a kid. She couldn't be sure because he rarely looked her in the eyes and seemed so shy. Although she thought he was kind of cute. He was also old back then. He was so scrawny, with hunched shoulders as well. What made her ask him to kiss her? Then, she was sure she was just flirting – wasn't she?

She could feel the solid muscles beneath his shirt. He had filled out so well. She wanted to giggle. He felt so nice and... When his thighs brushed hers and seemed to linger she forgot about giggling.

"Jake…" And now she couldn't move. He was holding her up completely. "Stop, right now. Just stop. What are you trying to do?"

"I'm not sure. It's just when I touch you I…" His voice trailed off and he grimaced. "You're right, I shouldn't be talking about this. It was always my little secret."

"I agree you shouldn't have told me. Especially now when you're c*onsidering* asking Tracy to marry you and we're neighbors." Sophie wondered how she would have reacted if he hadn't hid his feelings back then.

"I always loved your smile Jake…" Sophie's voice trailed off. Oops, maybe she shouldn't have said that out-loud.

"Ah ha. Now we're getting somewhere." And Jake pulled her closer if that was possible. They were almost standing still now and she could feel every inch of his body. She couldn't look up into his face. "We're sharing secrets. I worshipped you and you liked my smile. I wonder why it didn't go any further."

"Jake," She hissed pushing at his chest, feeling the heat, drowning in urgent need. She wanted more and didn't know how long she could behave. "Why did you ask me to dance?"

"You wanted to dance. I wanted to see you happy." Jake's voice sounded lame to her. "I wanted to let you know there are still guys around who want you Sophie. Now it's your turn to tell another secret."

No, no, no. She couldn't just let him keep talking to her like this. Did he like having women fight over him? He claimed he was helping, but what about his ego? Was he trying to pay her back for not remembering him? Really, she didn't know anything about who Jake was now and didn't then either.

"Oh look, Molly's here." Sophie didn't know that, but she prayed it was so. She couldn't stay here and listen to another word. Why the hell did Jake go and say that? He worshipped her from the time she was a teen and he wanted her. Then he was going to ignore that and marry Tracy. "You have issues Jake."

"Tell me what they are," Jake whispered in her ear. But he let her go and they walked back to the table.

Fortunately Molly had arrived, a little older and somewhat plumper. Sophie patted Molly's protruding tummy, before the two girls engulfed themselves in a big hug.

"Sophie, you haven't aged at all. A little Dorian Grey going on?" Molly stepped back and looked Sophie over. "Meanwhile I..." She patted her own belly, but with no malice. Ryan immediately slipped his arm around her waist, kissing her cheek.

"Yes, I sold my soul to the devil." Sophie sat down with Molly, falling right into the silly banter they always shared. "But you will have two kids, Molly. Lucky you. I want a baby so badly-" Her voice trailed off.

Turning she noticed Jake and Tracy in a heated, quiet discussion on the other side of the small table. It didn't take much to realize why they were arguing. Why had Jake held her so close? Did Jake want both women? He was so quiet and shy. Nothing made sense.

"I'm sorry Dennis-" Molly grabbed her hands. Sophie looked at her with a frown. It was rare she thought of Dennis other than realize it was a fortunate escape. She would tell Molly she wasn't heartbroken, but not here in the bar.

"-dumped her?" Tracy's voice dripped with glee. Startled by the interruption, Sophie looked at Jake to see his reaction. Didn't he see Tracy had trouble being nice? Jake squirmed in his chair, looking uncomfortable.

"Dennis didn't dump Sophie. She dumped him." Jake inserted. Then his eyes dropped to the drink he was holding. Tilting the glass he downed the contents. "I was there."

"Okay Tracy assuming he dumped me, why do you sound so happy?" Sophie refused to show the indignation eating at her stomach. She didn't expect to hear such rude comments here in Crystal Ridge.

"With the way men fall over themselves for you," Tracy gave Jake a resentful glare before continuing. "I'm surprised one dumped you."

Jake grimaced when he stood. "Enough, Tracy. Come on I'll take you home."

He turned to smile at Sophie before they left. Yes, Jake had issues. Empathy seeped in when she thought of little boy Jake, abandoned and growing up with drunk Angus. Obviously he believed logic and a reasonable plan would happen without love. He told her Tracy would be an excellent rancher a wife. What did he think now Tracy was showing her true colors? But his reasons didn't sound much different than her motives for marrying Dennis.

"Trouble in paradise." Molly chuckled and turned to Sophie. "Thanks for bringing out her true nature in front of Jake."

"You're still the same," Sophie burst out laughing. Molly's comments sounded blunt but always made her giggle.

"Well, it's not very pleasant, making small-talk with her when they come to visit." Molly continued. "And she won't even play cards. Will she Ryan?"

Ryan shook his head with a small reprimand. "I'll never understand women. You're as rude as she is."

"What? It's my fault she won't play cards?"

"Stop it." Ryan grinned to soften his command. "It is the first time Tracy's shown Jake that side of her nature. She really hates you Sophie. I wonder why."

"She was so jealous of Sophie. I saw it all the time." Molly explained. "Maybe she wanted Jake, even back then. And we all know Jake could only see Sophie."

"We didn't all know." Sophie denied. "I never knew."

"Rumor had it you two did a lot of riding together - alone. You're the reason Jake was out at the Dawson place all the time." Molly slanted a mischievous look at her then continued. "Rumor has it you guys have started that up again."

"Molly!" Both Ryan and Sophie spoke in unison.

"I didn't start it. It's so noisy in here. Let's get out of here."

Molly chuckled. "The Esso is open."

"You're upset because you can't have a drink." Sophie teased. She stood. It was so noisy it was difficult to hear unless someone was whispering in her ear. She squelched that thought immediately.

Streets did roll up by nine in Crystal Falls. Stores had dim lights in their windows and doors locked against intruders. A few streetlights scattered along Main Street looked isolated and out of place in the darkness. The Esso out on the highway remained open for the night travelers.

They drove out in Ryan's truck. A bright lit interior and a half dozen chrome tables were scattered around the small room. The Esso was simple with no atmosphere. A long counter with perky red seats brightened the gray walls and tiled floor.

She wondered what conversation was taking place with Jake and Tracy. Was Tracy able to have a conversation without complaining? Did she complain all the time? As things stood, she knew Tracy shouldn't have any worries or concerns. Sophie refused to be Jake's play-toy until he got around to asking Tracy, the perfect woman, to marry him. What a jerk. Inside, her heart mocked her thoughts. Jake might be confused but he wasn't a jerk to her mind.

Midnight crept up before the three went home. The porch light glowed cheerful in the darkness but her mother was in bed.

. . .

Something inside held Jake back from telling Tracy to go to hell. He despised her behavior towards Sophie. But he couldn't rid himself of the idea she would make a loyal, good wife and that Sophie never would. He parked in front of the only apartment building in Crystal Falls then went around to help Tracy dismount. She clung to his arm, smiling up into his face.

"Come in for a tea? It will help you sleep."

Jake groaned. No he didn't want tea. He wanted to go home and dream of Sophie, holding Sophie, touching Sophie. With determination he pushed his thoughts away. It was a though he was a teenager again. Sophie was a dream to cherish, not reality. He turned to Tracy and nodded. He needed to talk to her.

"Tracy, why do you hate Sophie?" He said blunt and to the point. Sitting with wary caution, he was afraid his weight might break her delicate couch. He had a sinking fear this was how his home would be decorated if he married her. Why wasn't life easy? Why didn't Sophie have Tracy's good qualities and Tracy have Sophie's bad qualities? Damn, he was stupid. When had life ever been easy?

"I'm sorry Jake, for being such a bitch." Tracy set the tea-cups on her French provincial coffee-table. She looked calm. "Sophie just has to go after another woman's man. It's a disease with her. She flirts with you because of me. Men can be so blind."

Confusion ran rampant throughout. Was Tracy right? His mother... Angry again, he pushed his thoughts away.

"Sophie's not like that. She never was. She doesn't have such mean, deliberate thoughts. Sophie just wants to have fun. When she was a teen and now, it's the same. But it's not Sophie I want to talk about. Tracy, you're going around town telling lies."

"I haven't." Tracy guided his hand to the teacup. "We've been dating for a few months now and I thought…"

"Thought what?" Jake shook his head. "We've dated a few times. That's it. I appreciate your cooking but I've never given you reason to think we're getting married."

"We've gone to Ryan and Molly's. You haven't dated anyone else."

"What if I did?" Jake felt surly and mean. Was he making a mistake if he let Tracy go? She sounded as though she was assuming, not lying. It wasn't as if no one else assumed things here.

"Jake think what you're doing before you go making a fool of yourself. You'll never be able to give Sophie the attention she needs. She didn't give you the time of day when she was in high-school. Why is she doing this now?"

But she did, his heart screamed in protest. You don't know. I can't tell you. It didn't mean anything. It was just Sophie, demanding attention, looking for excitement. Like his mother, Sophie needed more attention than any normal man was able supply. And she'd ignored him in the past except that one day. Hell, she willing admitted she didn't remember him when they met at Ranchman's. But she had only been a young girl back in high-school and she noticed him now. He shook his head trying to clear his maudlin thoughts. He needed to determine what to do about Tracy, not make excuses for vibrant, beautiful Sophie. Where Sophie was concerned he couldn't think straight. But his reason for needing a wife like Tracy was a more necessary plan.

Perhaps he should have a fling with Sophie and then when she moved on, come back to Tracy. He was not pleased with his callous, despicable reasoning. That would be unfair to Tracy.

He straightened. "Tracy, if we're going to continue dating you have to drop that attitude you have towards Sophie. You don't know her at all. So stop judging her."

"I'm sorry Jake." Tracy looked ready to cry. "I'll try to be more pleasant. But..." She hesitated only for a moment. "I agree, I was being unreasonable, thinking Sophie was interested in you. She wasn't before and there's no reason she will be now. Maybe she can't help the way she flirts with everyone, not just you."

Jake nodded and stood. "I need some sleep. There's a lot of work to be done tomorrow."

"And I'll come out to cook you dinner tomorrow night." Tracy looked hesitant again. "I really am sorry Jake."

'*We'll see*,' Jake wanted to say, but didn't. He really needed some time to straighten his chaotic thoughts.

Chapter Eight

Sophie woke to a gentle shake and her mother's voice. The sun streamed in through her window again. She pulled the pillow over her face to block out the light. A thought filtered through her sleepy haze. She bolted upright.

"Mom, do you have Jake's number? I have to call him to tell him I'm late. He can just go to work. I can go by myself."

"You and Jake are together too much sweetie. You shouldn't be bugging the man." Alice shook her head, but didn't say anymore.

"Mom, I told him he didn't need to ride with me." Sophie started to explain. The look her mother gave her was revealing. Did people think, even her own mother, that it was her fault men stared at her or wanted to be with her? Should she change her whole personality and appearance? Was she supposed to lock herself away and become a recluse or nun?

"Jake said he hasn't asked Tracy to marry him." Sophie flushed, feeling guilty and not knowing why. "He just comes riding with me. I didn't ask him."

"Well, one of them is lying." Her mother's voice was soft. She patted Sophie's shoulder. "You're right, Jake doesn't lie. But Tracy must have a reason to believe Jake is going to ask her. That isn't why I woke you. Dennis is here to see you Sophie."

Sophie flopped back and pulled the pillow to cover her head again. Dennis? She didn't want to see him. It had taken ages to fall asleep. Her thoughts were on Jake and trying to accept he made his choice. It wasn't her. Then why did he keep kissing her as though he had no control over the matter? And that dance last night. What did that mean? She truly believed Jake didn't know what he wanted, only what he thought he wanted.

"Tell him to go away." She mumbled beneath the pillow. But, just as her mother taught her long ago she knew she must face the problem and resolve it.

She put on a pair of jeans and a tank top, knowing it would probably be another hot day. Very rarely did it rain in the summer here. Already the sunshine was streaming warm through her bedroom window. She splashed some water on her face and brushed her teeth ignoring her hair. It was growing out awkwardly and she really needed a cut to clean up the mess. Hair poked up everywhere. Not long, not short.

Going down the creaking, wooden steps she thought she might need to help her mother with some repairs. Things were falling apart.

Dennis was sitting on her mother's flowered easy chair, looking very grim. Her heart sank and then fluttered with anxiety. She walked into the living-room as casual as she could, trying hard not to scream.

"What could bring you so far from your precious work?" *...And Liz'*, she wanted to add but didn't. Sitting down on the couch, she noticed her mother had a coffee-pot and cups sitting on a tray. She reached over to pour herself a cup and looked up at Dennis.

"You know I stopped drinking coffee." His voice was critical. He sat back in the chair and crossed his legs. "What are you doing Sophie? It's not like you to be so..."

His voice trailed off, but she could hear the scorn in his tone as he perused her tousled figure.

"Why didn't you just text?" Sophie couldn't help the feeling of shame flooding her body. Dennis didn't tolerate sloppiness well. She forgot how he could make her feel. Standing, she went over to the huge window to stare out into the neatly manicured yard. "Why did you come out?"

"You know damn well you aren't answering your texts." Dennis sneered.

Again with the accusations. Her body stiffened. She knew Dennis very well and also knew she couldn't let his derogatory comments bug her.

"I'm sick and tired of a texting relationship?" She turned to glare at him.

"You're so childish and demanding Sophie." Dennis sighed as though he was the one scorned.

Sophie wanted to laugh, but knew that would only increase his superior attitude.

"I tried to tell you but you wouldn't listen. Liz kissed me, I didn't kiss her and it meant nothing." Dennis said.

"Sure… and pigs fly too." Sophie turned again so she didn't need to watch his lying face. It sure looked like he was kissing Liz and there was nothing wrong with her eyesight yet. "Look Dennis it is over. Accept it and move on. Neither one of us is heartbroken."

"And what about the wedding?"

"Pat will still be getting married. The money won't be wasted." Sophie felt bitterness seep in. This was so typical Dennis. He didn't want the money to go to waste.

"And the business? We have clients expecting…"

"Stop it Dennis." Sophie was angry. She went to sit on the couch again. "Hire someone. There are loads of computer experts looking for work. And as you said yourself, I'm easily replaced. Remember? I think it was right around the time you were calling me conceited."

"I did not…" Dennis looked about ready to stand and strangle her. Then he sat back and continued. "Look, you have an obligation. Its part your company too. And it should be you vetting a replacement."

"Send them out here and I'll vet them." Sophie suggested, sarcastic and firm. "Look Dennis, I'm not going back. I don't like what I was becoming and obviously you don't want to marry me. That's fine. You're only interested in the bottom line and squeezing us for money. I see that. Maybe as Liz is an accountant she'll share your dreams. I wish you all the happiness. I have a computer here. Until you hire someone else, just send the work to me. I'll see your clients are happy. But get someone to replace me as soon as possible."

"And your shares of the company?"

"Get your people to contact my people..." Sophie did laugh then, always wanting to say that ridiculous statement in the right context. "Seriously, I don't have a clue what my shares are worth. I trusted you. But maybe that was a mistake. Figure out what you owe me, I'll get a lawyer to look at it and if it's right, buy me out."

"It's not as though we have a cash flow..." Dennis started. "We can't really afford to buy you out right now."

"You mean my shares might be worth that much?" Sophie gasped in surprise. "Then why on earth were we living so miserly? Or at least I was. Forget it Dennis. I don't care. Just send me the client's information you want me to do until you find your replacement. I don't need the money right now. I'll just remain a silent partner for now."

"No, you have your mommy to sponge off again." Dennis stood. He was condescending. Just like always. Sophie realized what a disaster it would have been if she had married him. It's not that Dennis was physically mean, but with his control issues he definitely needed to feel it was his generosity that gave her a good life.

She didn't bother informing him she was helping Ryan, until she got her thoughts in order. He would only ridicule her for that too. Imagine his thoughts on her working as a waitress with her qualifications. She walked to the door, opening it.

"Bye Dennis."

"I told Pat you were just an empty box with pretty wrapping and she's beginning to agree with me." He didn't bother looking at her. He just got up off the chair and walked to the door.

What a cruel man he was. She felt a combination of relief she wasn't marrying him and sadness wondering why she'd stayed so long. What a waste of time. But the pain that Pat could break up their life-long friendship was inside too. She had the strongest urge to call Pat and talk. Maybe if Pat heard the horrible things he said when he was angry, Pat might not be so willing to judge her. She realized he'd always make his awful comments at those times no one was around. But Dennis was Pat's brother and she understood why Pat would want to be loyal to him.

She watched Dennis get into his car. He made no further comment. It was obviously over. She didn't want to prolong the visit. Sorrow crossed her thoughts. The grief of something she thought was there but in fact wasn't.

"Well he didn't appear too heartbroken." Her mother set a cup of coffee down on the kitchen table when Sophie moved to the doorway. "I don't think that boy likes it when his plans are thwarted."

"Exactly." Sophie muttered. After moving the tray to the counter she sat down and drank from her own cup. "You don't know the half of it. But it's Pat that I'm wondering about. Will this end our friendship?"

"It shouldn't and I hope it's not going to." Her mother threw her a sympathetic look, getting up to load dishes into the sink. "You two were always together."

"She texted me a few times to say she never wants to talk to me again." Sophie offered as an explanation.

"Well that's a good sign." Her mother stated lightly, running the water and adding soap. "If she really didn't want to talk, she wouldn't send texts, now would she?"

Sophie smiled. It was odd how many messages she'd received and not answered. Maybe she should send one back instead of ignoring them. It would have prevented today's disastrous start.

"I agreed to work on websites, until they find someone to replace me." Sophie changed the subject.

"Will you have time? I thought you were working for Ryan. You were gone all day yesterday."

"I was only there because Trudy wasn't there and Ryan was busy. I went for a drink with Ryan and Molly. Ryan's mainly going to teach me to cook and asked me to work when Trudy can't come in. He said he was stranded yesterday. He was busy. He wants to spend more time with Molly, now she's pregnant again."

Alice laughed. "Good luck Ryan. You were always so absent minded whenever I tried to teach you to cook. You found every excuse in the book to go outside and help your dad. How is Ryan's teaching going?"

"Not so great. I like food well enough, just the cooking never seemed to catch my interest. I know how to make Eggs Benedict now." Sophie brightened. "Dennis asked what I wanted to do about my portion of the business. What do you think mom? Maybe I'm worth something after all."

"I taught you better than to judge yourself by what you're worth in money. The company has been going for ten years now and it appears to be successful." Alice came to sit at the table. "Well, I guess if it appears Dennis is screwing you, maybe Rick Larson can help." Rick was Crystal Ridge's only lawyer.

"He's too honorable to screw me. But I was wrong about him before. We'll see. He put a check in my account. It's not like I don't have money right now. Living with Dennis, I saved a lot of my wages." Sophie said lightly. Then flushed and dropped her eyes still not comfortable discussing her living arrangements with her mother. "Mom, I should hire a contractor to fix a few things."

"Yes, I've been meaning to do that," Alice sighed, looking around at the neglected house. "I don't seem to have much left over, with only pensions now and Jake leasing the land."

"We can use the money I'm getting from the business. I'll ask Dennis to give me a figure. You could do it anytime you want. I'm sure I have enough in my savings. Is there a construction contractor in town?"

"Yes. I'll call Dave and see what he says." Alice nodded, taking another sip of coffee. "I'm busy now. The CWO is planning their annual bake-sale and dance, raising funds for the hockey teams. But in September we could get him to start working."

"When is the bake-sale?" Sophie recalled her mother's participation in the past. Then it wasn't important. Randy's parents had enough money to pay for Randy's hockey, but now it was different.

"It's Labor Day long week-end. The same time as the fair."

She told her mom about Dominic wanting to play hockey.

"Oh yes. I always feel so sorry for that family. Millie has four kids and Jim is a real lazy drunk." Alice sighed. "It's almost as though there's something in that house. It was Jake and Angus' house. But at least it was only the two back then. I can't imagine having six people living in that shack. I wish we could do more."

"Well, I understand you ladies give donations of clothes to poor families," Sophie patted her hand. Her mother was always busy with her Catholic Woman's Organization. Sophie was happy to see Alice still had a full, busy life.

"I figured out a way to help Dominic, mom." Then she told her about Ryan's plan and how she was going to pay for the hockey equipment for Dominic.

"That's a good thing, if you can afford it. You're a good, generous girl." Alice smiled just like a proud mother would. "Sophie, I only give you advice, not criticism. I hope you know the difference."

"I know mom." Sophie got up to hug her mother. "I know when all the world is against me I can count on you. You taught me that and I'm always so grateful knowing that."

Chapter Nine

Sophie was driving him crazy, Jake realized. Yesterday she hadn't shown up for her morning ride and Jake couldn't believe how disappointed he was. In the restaurant with Tracy was a disaster. He sat silent and let Tracy make outlandish remarks that weren't true. He felt sorry for Tracy, she was so obviously trying to warn Sophie to stay away. He wasn't sure what to do about that either. Tracy promised she wouldn't say anything more.

He groaned as recalled that certainly in the bar he'd made nothing but a fool of himself. He just couldn't stand the idea that Sophie might dance and be attracted to someone else. He was jealous when he didn't have any right to be so.

Unlike Ryan's successful coffee-shop, Jake's dreams of a ranch were just dreams so far. The struggles and belief he could succeed were fast disappearing in a mired mess of financial problems and work that said it might not be possible. He was just hanging on, nothing more. The harder he worked, the less profit he made. He couldn't hire more men because he didn't have the money so he tried to do the work himself.

Then like a ray of sunshine, Sophie appeared for her morning ride. All his thoughts disappeared as he considered how he could kiss her. He knew he should tell Tracy he wasn't going to ask her hand in marriage. He was falling so hard for Sophie that he was even considering accepting her flighty ways just for the days of happiness she would give him. He was a dupe and had to get a grip on reality.

"Hi." Even her voice was a light whisper of promised delight for that short time she would stay with him. He knew he would be in paradise.

"Hey, I know you have lots of work so I can ride on my own. Really I can."

She looked so frail and helpless and he knew he couldn't let her ride on her own.

"I hope you didn't wait too long yesterday. Dennis showed up and it was too late." Sophie continued. "I forgot to call you. Well, I don't you're your number but..."

"Dennis came? What for? He's trying to convince you to go back to Calgary?" Jake interrupted, surprised at the fury licking inside.

"Of course not. Dennis is going to marry Liz and he will probably. I bet he'll even keep the same day we were supposed to get married, so as not to waste money. He hasn't told me that yet. I should call Pat if she'll talk to me. I'm just going to do a few web designs until he finds someone else."

Sophie studied Jake's lean, tense form. "Boy, you really aren't very pleasant in the mornings are you?"

Only Sophie would say that, blunt and to the point.

He looked up and grinned. Sophie gave a small gasp. He knew his smile probably revealed it all. He was so happy to see her. Sophie thought he belonged to Tracy. Tracy said so and Jake didn't deny it. It was safer to have her believe that. But he could feel Sophie's attraction and he wiped the grin off his own face knowing it held the same emotions hers did.

He watched her tremble when she picked up Betsy's reins.

"Tomorrow, can I ride Sage again?" Even her voice was quivering as she swung into the saddle. "He just caught me by surprise. If I can ride him can I please just go alone? I feel so guilty."

'And I feel so guilty, because even knowing I should be working I want to ride with you', Jake thought but didn't say out-loud. No wonder his ranch was failing.

. . .

After her ride, Sophie took her mom's truck into town again. Ryan wasn't busy so instead of teaching her how to make meatloaf as she requested, he suggested she take Dominic into Calgary to get his hockey gear.

"Use my pick-up. I don't know if your mom's will make it," Ryan suggested casually.

"I was thinking I should get a new vehicle. How are Sean's prices down at Varsity? Or should I get a vehicle in Calgary?"

It was only just over a hundred kilometers into Calgary but it was into a whole different world. It was Saturday and another hot day. Dominic, after gaining his mother's approval, was ecstatic. She wanted to ask him how often he had been outside Crystal Ridge, but knew he might be embarrassed and defensive. She didn't want to destroy his day.

She drove to South Centre shopping mall. The parking lots were packed. Something she'd forgotten. She enjoyed Dominic's enthusiasm and company once they got inside the sports store and he started picking out his gear. Dominic was worried about cost until Sophie assured him he had enough. His little shoulders relaxed and he started picking out things he liked and wanted. The young sales-clerk helped make sure he had proper gear. The bill was nearly a thousand dollars. Sophie insisted on buying him a big new bag to carry his equipment in as well.

"I got one last year." Dominic argued. "It's barely used. Well it was Jake's, but he said he didn't play much either so it was almost new."

So Jake did know Dominic better than he insinuated and he cared about Dominic's desire to play hockey although he didn't say. It warmed her heart. She didn't want Dominic to feel inferior about anything.

They stopped at Tim Horton's for Sophie's much needed fix of coffee. Crystal Ridge didn't have a Timmy's and she really missed their coffee.

Dominic filled up on donuts and juice. She couldn't summon the desire to stop him, sure this wasn't what he ate every day.

"Hey, you lived here. How did you ever find your way around?" Dominic was watching the traffic outside carefully but looked confused and apprehensive.

"Just google it." Sophie laughed, passing him her I-phone. He picked it up as though it were a piece of gold and eyed it. She leaned over and turned it on. "Just type in an address and it will take you there."

Dominic carefully typed in places, like the Zoo or Heritage Park and was delighted to see directions on how to get there.

"Hey, I got a question for you that I'm trying to figure out," Dominic's enthusiasm was contagious.

"Ask away." Sophie leaned over the small table and ruffled his hair with affection.

"Mom just laughed when I asked her, but if Jesus is the sun, does that make God the moon?" He looked puzzled.

Like Millie, Sophie laughed. What a wonderful, inquiring mind he had. Millie must be so proud. Then she sobered and solemnly gave him a lesson on spelling and the difference between son and sun. Dominic nodded and grinned.

"That makes sense. Didn't want to ask the teacher. I have enough problems without being dumb too."

Sophie's heart melted into a puddle of love. What a precious boy. She wanted to ask him what problems he was having at school, but noticing his ease with her, decided not to push him. She discussed hockey instead, quite sure it was probably his favorite subject. Dominic was animated, flinging his hands around, trying to express himself. His poorly done hair-cut caused his sandy hair to fall into his eyes. She wanted to take him for a haircut but knew he wouldn't accept her offer. Finally, she stood, deciding it was time to go home although she was reluctant to end the day.

Then Sophie decided to buy donuts for Dominic to give his whole family. Again, when he pulled a few more coins from his pocket, she let him believe he was paying for this very special treat too. The pride in his expressive face was tangible. She felt so happy he was having a good time.

By the time they got back to Crystal Ridge it was getting dark. The sun, setting below the mountains created that charcoal and pink sky.

"There, the exact colors I want in my bedroom," Sophie gasped with delight. She never tired watching these amazing sunsets.

"Sure wish I could get it for you," Dominic whispered. There was complete worship in his tone although she was sure he didn't understand what she was saying. She wanted to cry and hug him, imagining this would be the feelings a mother might get from her children. It was the most wonderful feeling she had ever experienced.

"You will be able to one day. Now it's time to play hockey. Maybe you'll get into the NHL." Sophie knew it was every boy's dream to do that. It had dominated Randy's dreams for many years.

"Oh yeah. I will. I'll try really hard. Then I can get you a pink and black bedroom, I promise."

Sophie tried to keep the tears from her eyes. Dominic displayed his adoration like a badge and she seriously doubted she could ever do enough to make his life easier. Dominic's pride said he wouldn't just take whatever she offered. She drove across the tracks and immediately thought *'the wrong side of the tracks'* wasn't just a saying in Crystal Ridge, it was a fact.

The old house was along a neglected street and Dominic's house was the most neglected. t was also the smallest. Dilapidated sagging wood shake, obviously burgundy color once by the chipped paint. It had a broken, cardboard covered window in the front and the steps leading to the front door were bare and sagging, looking as though they had never been painted. The house appeared gloomy and forlorn in the dimming light.

Sophie had to hug him when she helped him out of the truck. He didn't fuss much. "Go give your mom the donuts and I'll carry your stuff to the porch."

Dominic rushed to the door that was opening. His beaming pride was a delight to see. And Millie responded with a real smile as well, waving at her.

Chapter Ten

The days were flying by. Between helping Ryan, or more like Ryan helping her, and doing the websites Dennis sent her, Sophie was busy. Her mom was gone nearly every day as the CWO organized their annual bake-sale and dance. Alice needed her truck and Sophie knew she had to get a vehicle for herself.

"Ryan can I walk down to Varsity now? I'll be back by lunch." It was Trudy's day off. Ryan had all the burdens of the lunch crowd as well as their coffee-break times.

"Sure, I can handle it. And here's Dominic to help."

Dominic came in with a huge grin. His expression changed to one of longing when he heard Sophie was going to get a vehicle. He picked up his broom without complaint.

Sophie came back with a fully loaded Dodge Ram 1500. She paid cash. She would have to tell her mother they might need to pay Dave in installments. Her savings were nearly depleted again, however she had income coming in both from Four Plus and from Ryan.

Regardless of how hectic she was each morning Sophie still walked over to Jake's barn and saddled Sage. She refused to admit how depressed she was now that she rode alone. Jake wasn't talkative, but she always felt comfortable with him. Let's face it, he was good company because he was so sexy and he was so good to look at. And she realized she was shallow to think that was enough. Jake was a kind and hard worker. It was apparent he didn't want people to see that side of him. Did he think it was a sign of weakness? And why couldn't she just accept that Jake said he wanted to marry Tracy.

August rolled in. The weather just baked the earth and Sophie knew Jake and his hands were moving the cattle to higher ground. She knew it was selfish on her part to be upset he couldn't ride with her.

As the days crept closer to her former wedding date, depression invaded seriously. She was so thankful she wasn't marrying Dennis. She wanted so badly to talk to Pat. Until one night, a few days before the wedding Sophie called her.

"Sophie? Sophie! I'm so glad you called." Then Pat's eager tone dwindled off to a faint touch of remorse too. "It's so hard to believe, you're not here."

"I feel the same," Sophie sat cross-legged on her flowered bedspread, twisting the material around her fingers. Staring at the flowers, she felt empty inside. "I wanted to be with you for your wedding. I'm sorry, I couldn't marry Dennis. You understand don't you Pat?"

"Well, I sure do now." Pat sounded very upset. "Sophie, Dennis is marrying Liz tomorrow. It will still be a double wedding. You had a reason to be suspicious of her. She's a real piece of work. I don't think I want her for a sister-in-law."

Sophie was laughing when she interrupted. "I told Jake-"

"Your cowboy is still around? You already got a new man?" Pat's voice changed to disappointment.

"Oh Pat. Settle down. Dennis is marrying Liz. What do you think I should do – waste away with unreciprocated love? Join a convent? Jake is Jake McCallum. Remember old drunken Angus? Well Jake is his son, that sad looking scrawny boy who didn't talk. Besides, Jake is engaged to Tracy."

"Tracy–the Tracy in class? No," Pat was laughing now as well. "Poor Jake. That cowboy who helped you was Jake? Dennis said he was a 'big' strapping man and he had no intentions of tangling with him."

"Well, he's much bigger than Dennis now. He filled out quite nicely. I wish he wasn't engaged to Tracy." Sophie said with some hesitancy. At one time she would have blurted out all her feelings to Pat. But times were different.

"Wow. You like Jake? Why is he engaged to Tracy? Has she changed that much?"

"Pat, she's a frumpy looking *house-frau* now instead of a weird Goth babe. But she still has the personality of a witch I think. She knows how to cook and apparently that's important to Jake."

"Well, if that's what Jake wants I guess you can't compete. Come on Sophie, don't let that little fact stop you. Show him you have other intriguing assets. He'll forget all about eating." Pat giggled, teasing her. Everyone knew Sophie didn't cook very well.

"I'll have you know Ryan is teaching me how to cook." But Sophie was smiling. She would never be in a chef category. She tried to imagine feeding Jake and his three hands. It was probably a full time, morning 'til night job. She wondered how soon she would get tired of that. But, maybe she wouldn't. There would always be the nights-

"Are you happy there Sophie?"

"Yes, yes I am." Sophie assured her. "It's easy to breathe here. And I can even disappear and be alone when I want. I never realized how much I was always with Dennis. I go over to the old Dawson place and ride a horse every morning. I can't even begin to tell you how much better that makes my whole day."

"I wish you were here Sophie. I really miss you." Pat said after what seemed like hours of talking.

"I miss you too."

"Why don't you come into town after the wedding? No one is taking any time off right now. We're just too busy. Oh, I do understand why you left the rat-race. But Bill promised we'd go in the winter—somewhere warm of course because we can't have a honeymoon right now."

"Make sure he sticks to that promise." Sophie stated lightly. "I might come in and see Dennis. He came out here and we talked about my shares. So maybe I'll make an appointment. Doesn't that sound silly, me making an appointment to see Dennis? If I let you know, can you at least go out for lunch with me?"

"I sure can. I'll cancel appointments for you." Pat stated immediately. "I'm glad you called Sophie. I miss you so much, but after those awful texts I sent, I was scared you'd tell me to go to hell."

"I know. It's the first time we've been apart." Sophie didn't want to hang up. But it was time. Pat must be hectic with work and arranging her marriage.

. . .

A few weeks later, after booking an appointment, Sophie sat in Dennis's office. Shock made her stare at the little piece of paper she was holding. Two hundred and fifty thousand dollars. She didn't expect this when Dennis agreed to see her only a few days after his wedding.

"It's only half," Dennis stated stiffly. She looked up. He was twirling a pen in his hand, staring down at his shiny cherry-wood desk top. He leaned back and swivelling slightly in his leather armchair. Dennis was exactly what he wanted to portray. He was the ultimate, sophisticated and successful man.

"Only half?" Sophie wanted to laugh. Now, she had more than enough to do repairs on her mother's house and buy her a good vehicle too. Then her thoughts moved back to the meager life Dennis had created for her. She even recalled the times he gave her a rough time for buying clothes. She looked at him accusing now. Was she unfair in believing she could have kept her apartment or car at least? Maybe with that bit of independence she might not have been so willing to run away?

Dennis shrugged and she caught a glimpse of hunger in his eyes. She knew that look so well. She gasped, wanting to say *'you've only been married a few days'*, but didn't. It was over and there was no sense carrying a grudge. Poor Liz. *'She had a lucky escape'*, crossed Sophie's mind with fleeting swiftness. Was Dennis that type of man? Good staid, reliable Dennis was looking for an affair, shortly after he married? It was hard to believe.

"I'll try to get the other half by Christmas. I'll be in Crystal Falls then. Mom and dad want to meet Liz." He cleared his throat, looking down at the papers on his desk. "Are you sure you won't come back to work?"

"Yes, I'm sure." Sophie still felt the urge to giggle as she pictured Dennis, her boss, chasing her around the desk. It was a comical vision. It was so odd how circumstances could change in a moment. She stood up and walked to the door.

"Sophie-" Dennis got up from his chair and came around to touch her arm when she stopped. "I've got a few interviews next week for a web-designer. Is there any possible way you could come to town and vet them?"

It was as though Dennis didn't want to let go. And she instinctively knew she couldn't be around Dennis anymore. It was all nice, thinking they could be friends, but reality said she didn't much like Dennis and possibly never had. His one redeeming feature was that he was Pat's brother. She shook her head and continued walking out, not looking back.

Pat was waiting in the reception area. Hopping up, she came and hugged Sophie, clutching as though they hadn't seen each other in years.

"Marriage suits you..." Sophie stepped back to look at her friend.

"Oh wow, you're letting your hair grow..." Pat laughed, tears in her eyes. "Come on, let's get out of here before Dennis notices I'm not going out to meet a client."

The two girls drove to Moxie's. Both barely noticed the food as they rushed to tell each other what was happening in their new lives.

"So, Tracy is the new best cook in town." Pat's blue eyes rounded in mock surprise. "What does your mom think of that?"

"I haven't eaten anything she cooked, so I wouldn't go that far." Sophie held back on her laughter. She couldn't imagine anyone being a better cook than her mother.

"You realize from what you've told me Jake might be just marrying her to have a cook around to feed him and his men." Pat added her wisdom.

"Funny that you mention that." Sophie looked up, startled. "He told her they would starve without her."

"Well, if he isn't quite engaged to her, take him. You know you can."

"You know I'm not like that." Sophie sighed. "But I don't think unrequited love suits me. I get so impatient. Maybe I'll see if there is anyone else around town." Now that was a thought that depressed her. She didn't want anyone else. She wanted Jake.

"Or come back and see what's around here." Pat advised. "I'll even go with you. Bill won't mind."

Neither girl wanted to leave, but Pat had an appointment. With the promise of coming to Crystal Falls for the fair and bake-sale, Pat left.

When she left the restaurant and climbed into her truck, Sophie felt as though she'd been released from prison. A loud breath escaped and she felt free and happy. Two hundred and fifty thousand dollars! The same amount again was coming by Christmas. She was rich. Shifting the truck in reverse to back out, she sped down Deerfoot Trail and was soon out on the highway. Putting the window down and cranking up the music, she sang along to the tunes. She might be speeding. She wasn't wearing a seat-belt and it felt good. It gave the touch of carefree freedom she needed. Turning down the highway that led to Crystal Falls, she felt like the eagle soaring overhead. Free.

It was August and it was hot with no sign of rain. The sky was clear, pristine blue with no other color except where the sun spit out rays of hazy, glaring yellow. Today was a perfect day.

She went straight home. Trudy was in to help Ryan today. She was surprised to see Jake's Silverado parked beside her mother's beat up truck. It was the middle of the afternoon. Why wasn't Jake working?

Entering the hall, only slightly cooler than outside, she sighed. At least it was shaded. She thought of going upstairs to change her dress, but was too curious as to why Jake was here in the middle of the afternoon. She could hear voices in the kitchen. Moving down the hall, she could hear what they were talking about.

"I'm sorry Alice," Jake was saying. "I just can't be sure I will make the payments. I'm already a month behind with Willows at the bank. Can you see if anyone else can lease the land? Maybe Shorty-"

"Shorty wants to buy it Jake. I don't think Luke would have liked that at all." Alice piped up. "We can't let him own all the land around here. It's a monopoly. Just pay me when you can."

"Alice, you're so kind, but it doesn't feel right." Jake answered. "But you're right. There are too many big ranchers pushing us little guys out."

Curiosity was immediately replaced by sympathy. Jake was in financial trouble. Her mother really didn't need the money now although she didn't know that yet. Sophie was rich.

She stepped into the kitchen. "I can lend you the money Jake." She reached into her purse and fluttered the check in the air. "Look... I'm rich."

. . .

Shocked and bewildered, Jake felt the absolute, horrified *"No,"* escape immediately. What the hell was she doing now? She was offering money just as though he was a charity case. He felt like a kid again. Humiliation flooded his thoughts. He felt stiff and awkward. He knew his voice was too harsh and blunt. Intense humiliation surged through his veins as he stood up, glaring at Sophie.

There she was, like she'd just stepped out of a fashion magazine. She was wearing a cute little black dress that revealed her perfect figure and long expanse of leg so well. Gold chains and gold hoops adorned the costume. Who wore black in the summer? Sophie did, that's who. And she could. The dress looked like it was made for her and it probably was. Her hair was starting to grow out and was tousled and spikey. Being Sophie it didn't look awkward, like it should. He wanted to take her and...strangle her or maybe ravish her, if he was honest. Once again Sophie was showing he could never be in her class. Now she, with careless unconcern, was offering to buy him like he was a piece of meat.

"Forget it Alice. I'll find a way to keep leasing your land." He stood and turned when he reached to open the door. He was looking both puzzled and determined when he looked back at Sophie. "I don't need charity and never did. I'll figure it out."

. . .

"Well, what did I do?" Sophie looked at her mother, wanting to laugh and cry. She never expected that reaction. "I know he's good for the money. Why did I offend him?"

"Cowboy pride? Remember Jake grew up in poverty. To him your offer was both unexpected and charity." Alice inserted gently. "I know your intentions were good and very commendable, but Jake doesn't want to feel obligated, especially to you. He thought he could get away from that situation once he grew up. Old man Dawson left him with some debts on the ranch. And Sam, Dennis's father, isn't making it easy I think."

"He told you that? Then why doesn't he take my money instead?" Sophie muttered, thinking he should just take the money and be grateful. Why was it complicated?

"That poor boy is so confused," Alice explained. "He just doesn't know what to do."

"Why would Jake be confused and why do you call a thirty-five year old man a boy. If he took my money he could get away from Sam." Sophie was now in a bad mood. Inside, she knew the answers. When Jake married Tracy things would be different. And maybe borrowing money from her would obscure his decision to marry Tracy. He knew of her obvious attraction and starting a married life with someone else might be wrong. "He's making it all too complicated. He can still marry his precious Tracy and borrow money from me. I wasn't about to put strings on it."

"Well, maybe you could stop the confusion he feels just by putting strings on it." And her mother's statement only jumbled her mind even more.

Was her mother suggesting she should say he couldn't marry Tracy if he borrowed the money? And why would she be so controlling? If Jake loved Tracy he should marry her. Was he so dense he needed a woman to order him around and tell him what to do?

"I didn't mean that." Alice stood to move the cups to the sink. "I meant that your putting strings on the money, might make his decisions in his mind much easier. Jake knows Tracy will make a perfect rancher's wife and will help him. But are they compatible? It's beginning to look not. He sure likes you though and I think he likes you as a person too, not just your looks."

"But I wouldn't make a perfect rancher's wife? I wouldn't help him?" Sophie was hurt. Here it was again. That insinuation, by everyone, that she was useless because she was pretty. It wasn't fair.

"I certainly didn't say that." Alice turned and moved to give Sophie a hug. "I know you'd make a better rancher's wife than Tracy. You were always so eager and happy to go with your dad. And he often told me how much you helped. Do you notice Tracy doesn't even like riding? I know she's a good cook, but there is more to being a rancher's wife than cooking. It's as though Jake doesn't want to believe you'd make a good wife. And that's where his confusion lies. Poor boy."

"There you go again." Sophie hugged her mother. At least her mother realized she wasn't useless. "Jake *isn't* a boy."

She went upstairs to change. Then going to the bank she deposited her check, wondering what to do with all the money.

Feeling like she desperately needed someone to talk to she stopped in to see Molly. She was disappointed to see Emma, their little two year old, was sleeping. But it was a good chance to talk to Molly. The kitchen was bright in yellows and white. The cupboards were galley style with an adjoining dining area. Molly's black wrought iron and glass table looked comfortable with the sunshine streaming in the window.

Molly made her coffee while Sophie explained Jake's reaction to her offer.

"For all your popularity you sure don't understand men do you?" Molly smiled, to lighten the blow. "I'm not trying to insult you."

Molly set a cup of coffee down and sat on the opposite end of the table with her own. Her sparkling eyes had lost some of their vivacity and there were dark rings underneath.

"Do you nap now?" Sophie was sympathetic. "I can come back another time."

"Don't you dare leave," Molly interrupted. "Do you know how long it's been since I haven't had to watch The Cat in the Hat or play princess? Talk to me Sophie."

"Well, if Jake is having problems, why wouldn't he accept my money?"

"I would think Jake has no desire to continue on as a charity case. Remember that's how he grew up."

"I know. But it's different now. I thought he wanted to make a success of his ranch."

"I'm sure he does. Some may think he got something handed to him, I heard him telling Ryan that old man Dawson left him a hefty mortgage. It's with Willows bank and I bet you know better than I, what a pain that man could be." Molly explained. "I could never figure out how Pat got away with what she did. Dennis was different. He agreed with his father on everything. Money was the end all - be all of existence."

"I got the impression Sam believed women didn't matter. I don't think Mr. Willows expected Pat to be anything but a useless woman." Sophie answered. The surprised look in her eyes was a revelation. Of course Dennis was like his father and that would explain so much. She and Pat spent more time at the ranch, than in the Willows mansion on the outskirts of town. "But why wouldn't Jake rather owe me the money than Sam Willows?"

"Because he's a man and a man wants to support his woman." Molly's voice deepened as she tried to mimic a man.

"I thought that changed when Ken and Barbie became the modern couple. Ken lives off Barbie's rich dad doesn't he?" Sophie grinned. "I heard that somewhere."

"I know." Molly tried to remain serious. "It probably doesn't happen so quickly out in these small towns."

"Is Ryan so silly?"

"He doesn't need to worry about it much. I find it very difficult to work right now and I don't have any money." Molly didn't sound at all upset. "Raising kids is very time-consuming."

"I envy you so much." Sophie interrupted.

And the conversation turned to raising children and the joy Sophie longed to experience.

Chapter Eleven

September flooded the hills and mountains, painted in gold and yellow as trees changed color. The morning air was now crisp and revitalizing. The fairgrounds on the outskirts of the town was bustling with activity. A short midway offered a few games of chance, from tossing coins into bowls, to shooting moving ducks. The prizes were gaudy stuffed animals, ranging from small, big or all sizes in between. Along-side the midway there were a few food carts, adjacent to a small Ferris-wheel, a roller-coaster and rotating tea-cups for the little ones. In the middle of a track was a small corral where Shorty had brought his tiny Shetland ponies for rides. There was also a short track laid out for go-cart rides. On the other side of the track men congregated to watch random displays of bucking horses. Closer to the arena, in the shade of ash trees, tables were lined up with baked goodies. Alice's bake-sale was finally a fact.

Beyond the trees was the hockey arena. Further along, St. Peter's church with its' tall bell-tower loomed over the trees. Beside the church was the community center, where the barn dance that evening would take place.

Sophie sat with her mother sipping coffee. The morning air was near freezing temperatures now. Sophie wore a jean jacket over her jeans and T-shirt. Later she knew they would be baking from the sun as nearly as the delicious baked goods they were selling. Enjoying the cool wind tousling her hair, she could almost imagine she was out for her daily ride.

Down the line of tables she saw Tracy already had a line-up of people. Tracy was wearing a beige dress with a full skirt. Her dark brown hair was pulled up in a bun at the top of her head. A beige cardigan completed her ensemble. At this distance, she looked like a frumpy old woman, right down to her laced oxfords with chunky heels. Pushing her malicious thoughts aside was not easy. Especially when Sophie saw Jake approach Tracy's table. Even the ranchers took this day off.

"I'll go get us some more coffee." Alice stood and throwing out the dredges of her remaining cup she threw her paper cup into a garbage bin.

Sophie nodded, still watching Jake. Dominic came running up to him. Jake tousled his hair and leaned over to listen. Dominic was animated and when they both looked over at her she smiled. Dominic was probably discussing their trip to Calgary. She saw Jake reach over to Tracy's table and hand Dominic something. Tracy was smiling too, but it ended when she looked at Dominic. It was so obvious Tracy didn't like children or specifically didn't like Dominic.

"Excuse me,"

Sophie turned to see Millie standing beside her. Two little girls, both dressed in faded pink dresses and worn thin black jackets, stood beside her. But their golden hair was carefully styled in ringlets and pink plastic butterfly barrettes held the hair back off their pixie cute faces. They looked a lot like Dominic. In Millie's arms a baby was bundled and sleeping. Sophie wanted to take the baby and cuddle him, but didn't know exactly how Millie would react if she asked.

"Hi Millie," She instead leaned over to arrange her mother's cookies, mixing her slightly burnt ones amongst them.

"I just wanted to thank you for all you're doing for Dominic." Millie's voice was shy and hesitant. "I'm sorry I didn't invite you in when you brought him home. Jim was feeling sickly and didn't want company. Thank you for the donuts as well. The girls couldn't believe their eyes."

"You are so lucky to have him." Sophie forgot to feel insecure. She adored Dominic.

"I know." Millie's voice lightened too. Sophie offered her a chair and smiled down at the two girls. "And these are…"

"Julie and Janet. They start school this fall. The baby is baby Luke." Millie took the offered chair. She pulled the blanket down and Sophie wanted to cry. He was beautiful.

Sophie could feel Jake arrive at the same time her mother returned. She stiffened. Was Jake still angry with her? She rode alone in the mornings and hadn't seen him since that day he left, so livid when she offered him money.

Jake went straight to Millie and scooped the baby out of her arms. "How's my little Godchild cuz? I've been so busy I haven't even come in to see him."

"Hey you two – why don't you take the kids over for some rides. Millie and I can talk a little." Alice offered, sitting down beside Millie.

"Oh, I don't…"

"We'd love to." Sophie interrupted grabbing Dominic's hand and beaming down at him. He answered her smile with worship in his own eyes. "Come on girls. You want to ride the roller-coaster? Bring the baby too Jake."

"You making my plans for the day, lady?" But Jake looked amused, not annoyed. "I never knew you were so much a control freak."

"There's a lot of things you don't know about me." Then realized she shouldn't have said that. Sophie looked down at her toes encased in her sandals. Sophie hated closed in shoes. "I'm sorry. You can stay here and watch the baby if you want."

"Still making my plans?" Now Jake was laughing, and she knew she was making it worse.

"Give me the baby." Sophie demanded. "He can't go on the rides anyway. You take the kids on the rides."

"Don't worry Sophie. I'm teasing. Let's just share our duties. A day at the fair sounds wonderful to me too."

Jake was in a good mood, laughing and talking to Dominic and the girls as they moved towards the rides. She held Luke as though he were the most precious thing in the world. When he opened his eyes, dark, mysterious blue, she wanted to cry.

Oh how she wanted her own little bundle. She felt Jake's eyes on her, but didn't look up. Now, she was sure he would be able to read her mind.

They went on the few rides, amidst laughter and shrieks. Jake and Sophie took turns holding Luke, although Sophie didn't want to relinquish him. It seemed right to give him to Jake. He liked kids and that knowledge made her happy.

Jake and Dominic tried their hand at winning stuffed animals for all three girls. Sophie noticed the sun was directly overhead. She suggested they eat something. She could see Millie and Alice were still chattering.

"Man, she's a bossy lady isn't she?" Jake asked Dominic, trying to be serious.

"Well, she knows stuff. She showed me how to get around Calgary." Dominic refused to acknowledge there was anything wrong with Sophie.

"Okay buddy." Jake tousled Dominic's hair. "I agree. That surely tells me she knows everything. Calgary is a big city. I'm hungry anyway."

Sitting down at a picnic table they were bombarded with questions as they munched on hot-dogs and French fries. People stopped to talk, some teasing, some with questioning looks in their eyes.

Christine, wearing a beige dress, nothing like her daughter's gown, stopped.

"When are you coming in for a dress Sophie?" Christine, Tracy's mother, and Crystal Ridge's local dressmaker stopped. She was tiny and some would say too thin, but looking as chic as she had in the past. A beige floppy hat protected her chestnut curls and carefully made up face from the sun. "Just because you're back in Crystal Ridge, doesn't mean you have to lose your sense of fashion."

Sophie knew her jeans and T-shirt were not very fashionable. She stood to hug Christine with one hand, holding the baby with the other. She turned to grin at Jake. "See, I'm getting to be a pro at this."

Jake didn't say anything, just nodded. She could see the appreciation in his eyes and she flushed. Adjusting Luke's blanket and giving him back his soother, she pretended she was busy. What possessed her to say such a thing to Jake? She felt like she was boiling.

She laid the baby on the table and took that moment to remove her jacket. The weather was getting hot.

Christine went into peals of giggles. Worried, Sophie chose that time to look at Jake. Was Christine laughing at the family picture they portrayed? Jake's eyes widened, then narrowed and she could see his sultry gaze clearly. He was staring at her chest. He looked up at her and his smile was breathtaking. No, Jake was no longer angry. Maybe it would be easier to keep him angry rather than this way.

"Oh." Sophie turned beet-red. She looked at her tight shirt with capped sleeves. It wasn't the fact it was tight, making Jake stare. It was the silly caption right across her chest. Aladdin's lamp with the words 'rub me' were visible without her jacket.

"Rub me?" Molly came to the table. "Oh Sophie. You haven't changed a bit. How many offers have you had so far?"

"None." Sophie wanted to put her jacket back on. Why did she do this type of thing? But both Christine and Molly were laughing. And Jake was… devouring her with a ravenous look, making her both uncomfortable and edgy at the same time.

"Pass me the baby sweetheart." Jake was biting his lip to keep from laughing. He was still staring at her chest.

With trembling arms, Sophie did that. Sweetheart? Jake was calling her sweetheart? What was going on?

Janet pulled her down to her seat again, demanding her attention. "I'm gonna look like you when I grow up, aren't I Sophie."

"Me too. Me too." Julie piped in.

"Oh, better. Much, much better. You have real blonde hair. Lucky you." Sophie played with their ringlets. Yes, these two little girls would definitely be pretty. She giggled and reached for Julie's pink elephant. "Can we trade?" She had a spotted little dog and a larger tiger. Dominic insisted he give his winnings to her.

When Sophie dared look at Jake again, he appeared nonchalant and was looking at the baby. There was a soft, approving light in his eyes when he looked up at her. How could anyone make her feel this way with just a glance? She looked over at Tracy, but couldn't tell what she might be thinking. It was too far away. Searching the crowds, she wondered if she and Jake looked like a couple enjoying the fair with their children. But here everyone knew Jake belonged to Tracy.

"I see Millie is signalling us." Jake interrupted her thoughts. "I guess it's time to take the kids back. She probably wants to leave to get the baby fed." He stood and told the girls to tag along. Dominic, like the responsible boy he was, took their hands and followed.

Sophie felt sad. Today Jake was friendly. She couldn't tell if he was still upset about her suggesting she lend him money. Did that mean he had moved on? Did she have the nerve to ask him? Liking the easy comradeship they shared today, she decided not to bring the topic up again.

"Come on Sophie." Molly was still standing there. "Let's get your mom and Millie some food too."

"He called me sweetheart?" Sophie looked at Molly then. "Why?"

"I think- Oh never mind." Molly shook her head. "It's none of my business."

"That doesn't sound like you Molly." Sophie begged. "Tell me."

"I'll make a bet Jake is not going to marry Tracy. That's all I'm saying." Molly quickly caved in.

The two girls moved back to Ryan's food stand, ordering some food. Sophie took it back to Millie and Alice. Then she could hold the baby while Millie ate. Instead of leaving them, Jake wrestled with the other three on the grass nearby.

Now, Sophie was close enough she could see Tracy was glaring.

After Millie left, Jake went with Slim, one of his hands, across the racetrack to watch a few of the men riding bucking horses. He didn't go to Tracy until it was time to pack up and go home. But he drove Tracy away without saying goodbye. Sophie felt down as soon as he left. She knew it was too late. She loved Jake. And that was creating nothing but heartache ten times as strong as anything she felt for Dennis.

Alice was packing up her stuff as well. Sophie helped, pretending everything was fine. But inside she wondered if she would want to stay in Crystal Ridge nearly so much when Jake and Tracy were married. She knew the answer was no and she was no closer to making a decision now as when she left Calgary.

. . .

Jake had a headache, listening to Tracy's hysterical voice. He tried to ignore her as he packed up Tracy's stuff. There was nothing left except containers and a few lawn chairs. Of course everyone in town knew Tracy was an excellent cook. But he knew it wasn't enough. How foolish he was to think he could spend his life with this woman.

"You stay away from her." Tracy's voice rose in frenzied demand. "She's just playing with you Jake. She ignored you before. Why is she after you now? It's because Sophie can't accept there might be a man who doesn't want her."

"Stop this Tracy. Does it matter?" Jake got into the truck as she climbed into the passenger seat. His head felt as though it was splitting open. Her shrill voice was a piercing offence to his ears. He just wanted her quiet. Turning on the ignition, he swung out of the graveled parking lot and drove to her small apartment.

Tracy refused to live with her mother. Tracy actually called her mother stupid. Why, Jake didn't know and she never told him. Christine was somewhat flakey, but certainly she wasn't stupid. Odd that he should think of that now. Odder still was the fact that he realized no one liked Tracy much. Not Molly, not Ryan and possibly not even her own mother. He felt sorry for Tracy, but feeling remorseful wasn't a reason to marry someone.

He helped her carry the empty container box into the cluttered place and just set them on the floor. Every spot on the tables was full of craft items, from macramé to needlepoint. Various dried flower arrangements were on the walls. And her windows were covered with bold flowery curtains in rainbow colors.

Tracy was still muttering when Jake took her hand and set her down on the swirl-patterned couch. He heard 'bitch' and sometimes 'red-headed witch', but he tuned her words out as best he could.

He cleared his throat and looked down at the beige carpet. "I think we should stop dating all together." He felt as callous as he now realized she was.

"Jake. You can't throw away a life-time of happiness for a fling." Tracy's voice trailed off. Her voice was lower. She started mumbling again. "I knew it. I just knew when that red-headed bitch returned you'd make a fool of yourself."

"This has nothing to do with Sophie and everything to do with you and me." Jake felt irritation build. It was a side of Tracy he'd never seen before Sophie's return. But he was fast realizing others had and he winced at his blindness. He realized he could talk until he was blue in the face and Tracy would still continue to blame Sophie. "I won't be asking you out again."

The last thing he wanted was a long drawn out argument. There was no discussion. So he stood and walked to the door and turned to look at her. "It's not your fault, it's mine. There were no promises made on either side. I'm sorry if you felt there was more."

"Jake please stay and discuss this. I've loved you since high-school. There has been no other. But Sophie – she's had so many guys, probably all lovers and she's just a little tramp." There was a sob in her throat, mingled with condescending criticism. Jake could only hear the criticism. Tracy hated Sophie and for no reason that he could see.

"Don't!" His order was abrupt and concise.

He felt like a cad when he walked out the door. Tracy, for the first time since he'd met her, was silent.

Chapter Twelve

The moonlight streamed from behind the black foothills, beams of silver washed over the charcoal colored trees as night settled in. The community hall was brightly lit and Sophie could hear the foot-stomping band as soon as she parked the new truck.

Alice got out, looking tired.

"You should have let me handle the table and clean up the mess. Then you could have just stayed home for a nap." Sophie threw her arms around Alice. They walked down the curved concrete path, lined with flowers and benches beneath Ash trees. Wrought iron lights, looking like lanterns were set alongside the path.

Alice perked up immediately. "Don't be foolish. I'm fine. It's just all the preparations. It happens every year. When it's over I just go home and relax on the verandah with a good book. After I see and smell my flowers for a few days I'll be as good as new. What you and Jake did helping Millie with the kids was nice. I bet that's the first time she's ever had a break."

Alice made a beeline towards her CWO friends, all standing near the refreshment and snack tables. She placed her own goodies with the others. Beside them, on the painted stage a group of five men with instruments were playing a medley of songs, tuning their instruments for the questionable acoustics of the hall.

Sophie smiled. It was all so country, all so charming, all so what she loved. She was content to be back. The rush of the city was a hushed and muted memory.

Would Jake ask her to dance again tonight?

She saw Ryan and Molly and went over to their table. Giving Molly a hug, she sat down. Jake, his three cowhands were sitting there as well. And Tracy. But Jake and Tracy weren't sitting together. What happened?

Sophie smiled as Jake immediately pointed to the three men "Slim, Cal and Boyd". She reached over the table to shake the men's hands aware Jake was watching her. The pensive stare in Jake's eyes made her self-conscious. She sat, clasping her hands together on her lap.

"I think your mom and her friends exceeded expectations. We're packed tonight for the dance and they sold pretty well everything at the bake-sale." Ryan piped up.

"So it should be a good year for our hockey team," Sophie reached to squeeze Ryan's hand. "Our little Dominic should do well this year."

Molly laughed and agreed. The three cowboys looked puzzled.

"You and Ryan have a kid?" Slim, the oldest, weathered and lean, spoke up slowly. He was grinning which created deep creases across his face. "Wonder why that rumor isn't public knowledge?"

"It's kind of their adopted son," Molly explained, and the three men looked more confused. "Ryan and Sophie are helping Dominic Reynolds fulfill his dream of playing hockey. I'm a little busy or I would be helping too."

"Oh yeah. Dominic comes out to the ranch sometimes asking for work." Boyd, a lanky middle-aged man, nodded. "Jake usually gets him to do something and gives him a few bucks too."

Sophie looked up, surprised. Jake flushed. Why hadn't he mentioned he was helping Dominic when she questioned him? Instead he insinuated he didn't have time.

"It was fine, until he gets Dominic to come in and help me." Tracy inserted, making Sophie wonder if anything made Tracy happy. Then she lowered her eyes as she realized Tracy's implications. It sounded as though Jake's house was her house too. Then why weren't they sitting together.

"What a careless child. No discipline whatsoever. I wouldn't raise my kids with no control like Mille does." Tracy continued to complain.

Jake remained silent, but he did not look very pleased either when Sophie raised her eyes to him. She stared at his face, trying to read something from his expression. He looked uncomfortable and upset. As though feeling Sophie's eyes on him, he shrugged.

"Tracy came out and graciously fed us poor guys once in a while. Otherwise we would live on canned beans." He supplied reluctantly. He looked down at his glass of beer, embarrassed. Jake obviously didn't like people knowing his business.

"And you're a fine cook, my darling." Cal Callaghan, a younger version of Slim, lean and lanky with ruddy cheeks, looked up from the chicken wings he was devouring. "You make better wings than these and they're pretty good."

"You just like food Cal." Jake's face lightened. "You should learn how to cook yourself."

"Like we got time." Cal laughed.

The lights dimmed. The music started making sense. People moved to the floor. Sophie did not lack partners tonight. She renewed old acquaintances and danced with Jake's cowboys. Cal tried to teach her the Irish Jig. She came back to the table out of breath and gasping for air, she laughed so much.

Molly and Ryan danced a few slow ones. But Molly was now gigantic and waddled with her back tilted and her stomach protruded. She was due any time. Neither Tracy, nor Jake danced. Tracy talked in whispers when she moved over to the vacated chair beside Jake. She leaned into him, clutching his arm. Jake didn't appear to be talking to anyone, including Tracy. He watched Sophie instead. She felt his eyes on her all night.

"If you wanna be happy for the rest of your life, never pick a pretty girl for your wife-"

When the band started playing, Jake stood abruptly and reached his hand out to Sophie. His touch was electric.

"Dance with me Sophie." His voice was almost strangled.

Amidst laughing and guffaws from the others sitting at the table Sophie wanted to sink into the floor. Those seated at nearby tables, joined in. Desperately, Sophie sought out her mother. She didn't want to look at anyone else. How could he do this to her? Her mother was smiling and clapping her hands to the catchy beat. They were the first couple on the dance floor although it filled up quickly.

"Did you pick this song out deliberately?" Sophie wanted to lighten the heavy, intense longing she felt inside. Perhaps it was time to move away from Crystal Falls and start a new life somewhere. She knew she could only turn into a bitter old lady, staying here. She didn't dare look at Tracy. Why did Jake keep doing this?

"No, I didn't pick it. I think Slim did." Jake whispered lightly into her ear. He was holding her too close. From the heat of his hand, to his hips brushing hers every time they took a step, it was excruciating. "I would willingly pick a pretty woman for my wife."

She tried pushing him back, but his arms remained firmly in place. Everyone around them were watching and smiling. They didn't look malicious or mean.

"What are you saying?" Sophie whispered. After he married Tracy would he still keep taunting her? "Jake, you have to stop this."

"Remember me, *'strong back and weak mind'*? My mind is too weak." Jake's voice buzzed like a bee, in her ear. It wasn't even slightly annoying. Tingles spread.

"What about Tracy?"

"I told Tracy we were over. Tracy thought there was more than just dating. There never was." Jake explained softly, sounding sincere. "Stop worrying about Tracy. I told you I thought she'd make a good wife, but I never told her."

"It doesn't appear she knows any of this." Sophie shook her head. She tried to stifle the hope in her heart. Was it true? "I guess I need to hear that with her present."

"I don't blame you. I didn't want arguments so I didn't contradict her much. Sophie she kept lying to you, right in front of me. I can honestly say I never asked her to marry me. I never encouraged her to think we were going anywhere but dating - unless she read my mind. Because I admitted to you long ago, I thought of asking her to marry me."

"What made you change your mind?" Sophie blurted out, hoping he would continue being honest. Getting Jake to talk was somewhat like being a dentist and pulling teeth.

"There is no difference between a wise man and a fool when they fall in love," Jake murmured, causing a sweet, excruciating thrill against her ear. Was he saying he loved her? She lost her courage completely.

"Sophie, I really need to talk to you." He stopped dancing and looked into her eyes. "Will you come outside with me?"

"What will people say?" Jake was making this so complex. He ran so hot and cold. Maybe he wanted to accept her offer to lend him money and all this had nothing to do with his feelings towards her.

As he led her outside, she looked at no one. The hall was crowded and dark, but she knew there would be people watching, including Tracy. What were people thinking? Did she care?

"You aren't going to kiss me again?" Sophie stopped dead in her tracks, wanting to find humor in the intense situation. "Tracy and I could never become sister wives you know."

Jake laughed and his laughter was genuine. His face crinkled in amusement. His eyes were smoldering. "What a good idea. I would have never thought of that. Weak mind and all. Don't worry, I just couldn't handle two wives anyway."

He led her to a small bench. It was quieter here. She shivered as the cool air caressed her bare arms. Tonight she was wearing a dress. Blue with off-shoulder collar it was swishy with a full, uneven hemmed skirt. After the intense heat in the hall it was cold. The street light created beams on the park bench. The enduring smells of honeysuckle from shrubs lining the path lingered in the fall air.

"Why does Tracy hate you so much?" Jake's question shocked her to silence. Direct and to the point. He took off his jacket and placed it around her arms. "It's more than dislike. It's obsessive and scary."

Sophie stiffened. Was it always her fault? It always seemed so and yet she couldn't ever understand what she was doing to make it so.

"I'm sorry." Jake put his arm around her shoulder and pulled her closer. "I worded that wrong. I'm not blaming you. I just want to understand what's happening. She was different, when you weren't around. I'm glad you came because I would never have known until it was too late."

"I don't know." She tried to think of one incident, any incident where she had slighted Tracy. "She was always like that even in high-school. She hated me. Do you remember what she was like when she was all Goth and gloom?"

"She watched me a lot and sometimes approached me. I don't want to sound conceited, but I thought she maybe had a crush on me. But she was just a kid. She told me she always loved me, even back then. I think she's jealous of you. Maybe that's why she hates you?" Jake's voice trailed off. The light from the streetlight reflected off his face. He looked bewildered and discomfited.

"Jake, would you really marry her knowing you didn't love her?" Sophie reached up to stroke his cheek. "If I hadn't come to town..."

"Possibly." Jake grimaced, pulling her closer. "I feel bad about that. I led her on, gave her the impression… Until you came and damaged all my best laid plans."

Was Jake saying he loved her again? Did she love Jake? All those feelings inside said so, but maybe it was just lust? It was hard to believe that Jake McCallum could turn out to be so sexy. And was that a reason to love him? No, her love was not all surface. For the first time in her life Sophie realized what love meant. It was his kind nature, it was the way his slow grin created havoc, the way she felt, so comfortable and secure.

And what were his feelings? Was it just lust for him? Her heart sank into her stomach. Queasy flutters erupted. Was Jake just another man, like all the others? She wanted to ask.

"It sounds like Cal will be disappointed." Instead, Sophie tried to lighten the atmosphere. Just because she wasn't sure she wanted to know the answer.

"That's true. That boy loves food."

"Boy? You should get together with mom. She calls you a boy." Sophie stated with boldness. She always felt she could say whatever she wanted with Jake. "What about us?" She held her breath and willed her words back. It was too new. She needed time to think.

"Well," Jake hesitated. "We'll have to see. Wanna date little Sophie?"

Sophie laughed and put her arms on his, leaning closer. It was exactly what Jake would say. But she wasn't going to let him off the hook just yet.

"And inside are you contemplating whether I would make a good wife without loving me?"

"You are blunt and to the point aren't you?" Jake squeezed her shoulder softly. "I don't think you have to worry about that. I have always loved you."

Sophie's breath caught in her throat. She liked his answer.

"I won't make a good wife so you won't ask me to marry you though?" She knew her voice sounded forlorn, but tried to get over the sinking feeling inside. Did Jake just want a fling?

"No. Remember I never said that, you did." He turned her face to him using his palms. His thumbs stroked her cheeks. "I meant I'm following my heart, not my mind because I have to. It's early in the game and we shouldn't rush. I never thought of what I'd do if you felt the same way."

"What is your heart saying Jake?" She reached up and turned his palm in to kiss it.

"Always in a rush, aren't you?" Jake just laughed instead of answering. "Did your mom never teach you the virtue of patience?"

It was more like she'd never seen the purpose of patience. Patience created so much wasted time. But inside her heart was singing. Jake was no longer dating Tracy and Jake was interested in pursuing a relationship with her.

"Wanna dance Jake. I've finally met the man of my dreams."

"Because I dance?" He was still caressing her and studying her face. He leaned forward to nibble her lips. He finally kissed her again.

"It's a rare man who likes to dance." Sophie stood up, slipping her arms into the sleeves of his jacket. She felt giddy and playful. "Yes, Jake. Because you dance. Now let's get inside."

Chapter Thirteen

The following morning, Sophie stiffened in wary shock when she saw Tracy standing at Jake's barn. She was holding the reins of two saddled horses. One was Sage. How did Tracy know she rode Sage? Did Tracy spy on her? Was Tracy a stalker? Sophie felt uneasy and wondered if she shouldn't check out the saddle. Last night Jake eluded to Tracy's obsessive hatred. Did he mean Tracy could be dangerous?

"Good morning, Sophie." When Tracy spoke, small puffs of vapour escaped. It was into September and the mornings were definitely cool now. Later today it would be warm again.

"Hi Tracy. Why are you here?" Direct and to the point, Sophie didn't feel the need to pretend. Tracy never faked her feelings towards Sophie. Now they were supposed to be buddies? Why?

"Jake told me I should get more exercise. I'm going to be a rancher's wife so I thought helping outside might help him." Tracy's demeanor was bright and cheery. She swung up onto old Betsy. She looked awkward and tight. Did she know how to ride?

"Jake thought I could go with you. We will be neighbors after all and should let the past go." Tracy continued when Sophie didn't say anything.

The blatant lie took Sophie aback. Poor Jake. How was he going to untangle this mess? She believed Jake before she would believe Tracy. She wondered about Tracy's state of mind and if she needed help. She could well imagine Tracy's reaction if she suggested such a thing. Should she talk to Christine?

"I thought you worked." Sophie said instead.

"Not until ten." Tracy actually laughed. Tracy worked at Sam Willows bank. "Banker's hours and all."

A quick look at the saddle cinch and Sophie mounted too. She had to hold her tongue in silence. What was Tracy up to now? Jake had told her last night it was over between him and Tracy, yet here Tracy was. A queasiness in her stomach made Sophie wonder if Jake had lied. She quickly pushed that away. It was Tracy lying, not Jake. Jake didn't lie, regardless of how bad he looked. She knew that. Tracy often lied.

Kicking Sage into motion, it wasn't very long before Sophie saw Tracy had no intentions of doing anything beyond walking her horse. For a moment she thought of galloping away and disappearing. It was obvious Tracy was not a rider. Sighing, Sophie returned to walk beside Tracy's plodding progress. It was surely the least enjoyable ride she'd ever experienced. Tracy couldn't hide her resentment although she tried very hard. Sophie hoped Tracy's talking helped relieve her of her resentment. Tracy seemed obsessed with all her past woes.

"Maybe, you didn't so much, but Pat was downright mean." Tracy finally acknowledged Sophie wasn't going to join in the conversation.

"Pat was never mean to anyone. I doubt you can name an incident where she was or where I was for that matter." Sophie did speak up then. Tracy's suggestion was ludicrous.

"She treated me like I didn't exist. You all did. I talked to Jake once and he agreed that there were..."

"It's the past Tracy. Can't you get over it? All kids can be mean." Sophie interrupted, feeling there was a need to defend Pat. But it was falling on deaf ears. Regardless of how she racked her brains, Sophie couldn't recall Pat being malicious. They often gnored Tracy. Tracy took that to believe they didn't like her? They weren't nasty about it. Well, Molly occasionally came out with some witty comments, but really...

"Yes, we should forget the past." Tracy's smile was taut and phoney. She kept looking at Sophie and dislike was predominant in her eyes. "You're right. You and Jake are friends, so I suppose I have to accept you as his friend."

Sophie wanted to say something, but bit her tongue. It appeared Tracy lived in her own world where reality had no place.

"I hear you're a good cook and do crafts." Sophie wanted to see if anything would animate Tracy. She might not be too far off thinking Tracy had a problem. From the doom and gloom that surrounded her, Tracy was always in a deep depression. Sophie knew she would talk to Christine. Or probably Christine knew and couldn't do anything about it. Tracy was an adult and could make her own decisions.

"Yes," Surprise entered Tracy's face. She looked suspiciously at Sophie. "And I hear you're not."

"No." Sophie chuckled watching Tracy's face brighten. "I can't get the hang of it at all. Ryan has taught me some, but it's still all Greek to me."

"Well, I could probably teach you as well I suppose. Isn't it odd how your mom is such a great cook and you aren't? And my mother doesn't know how to boil water."

Tracy couldn't help but get her digs in.

Carefully, Sophie hid her thoughts. "But your mom is such a great designer of clothes. Maybe that's where you got your gift for crafts?"

It was Sophie's turn to be surprised. Tracy talked about crafts with affection and fondness. Sophie just listened, bored to death. But at least Tracy wasn't so hostile and that was a blessing.

It was difficult trying to cheer Tracy and Sophie wasn't going riding again with her. Even though she lightened up, Tracy still felt it necessary to make derogatory comments about everyone. While Sophie could care less what others were doing, it seemed of utmost importance to Tracy.

She was happy when Tracy suggested they turn around and get back to the barn. Her head was spinning and ached by the time they departed ways. Maybe she'd best start changing her habits. If Tracy was coming to ride in the morning she would be better to ride at night. Immediately guilt flooded inside. Once again, as an adult she thought of ways to avoid Tracy. She tried to imagine what it would be like to be Tracy, but couldn't. Instead of worrying and complaining, she knew she would move on to something else. And definitely not talk about everyone else's faults.

She went home and spent the day helping her mother clean up. Dave, the contractor, had started working on the house. He was doing the outside first, putting on a new roof because there was a leak in the attic. He was also installing new windows. The old ones weren't sealed too well. He wanted to get that done before the snow came. Then he would come inside to do the renovations in the interior.

"Mom, I'm going to watch Dominic's first game tonight. Do you want to come?" Sophie put her feet underneath her on the flowered sofa. Her mother was still in the kitchen, puttering.

"No, I'm going to read a new book." Alice came to the kitchen door, drying her hands with a tea-towel. Her eyes still looked weary. "I'm recuperating. Did you have a good time at the dance?"

"Yes." Sophie felt her head go into the clouds, as she danced with Jake. It was surreal, not tangible. Especially since her ride with Tracy. Had she dreamed last night? Was it true? Did Jake love her?

Sophie wished she could talk to Jake again. He said one thing and Tracy said another. Sophie knew she would sound like a clinging shrew if she continued to question him. But why was Tracy still there at his ranch? Was Jake too kind to tell her to get lost? Did he even know Tracy went riding this morning? Jake had told her last night he would have a busy September. It was time to bring the cattle down from the high-ground. And they needed much more feed piled for the winter. She offered to help, but he just smiled and ignored her. It was frustrating. Was Jake going to treat her like some silly bimbo too? Couldn't he see her as a person? And why wouldn't he talk about her lending him money. It was just another topic he ignored.

"Mom, I can afford to get you a car too. Do you want to go to Calgary and get one?" Sophie decided not to overthink her problem. The relationship she had with Jake was new and just starting. She had no idea where it might lead. "We should get one before the winter."

"Are you closer to making a decision? Are you going to stay here?" Alice leaned over to the coffee table, pouring more tea.

"I'm not positive but it looks like I will." Sophie prayed it would be so.

"And your relationship with Jake?" Alice continued, not even slightly tactful. "What's happening?"

"Mom, I don't know. He told me he broke up with Tracy. He's not dating her anymore. But today she came to ride with me and acted like it's still on."

"Poor Jake." Alice sighed, but said no more.

"Mom, I can afford to get us both a vehicle." Sophie went back to her original topic. She barely had time to absorb the situation herself, let alone discuss it with her mother.

"I know dear. But if you're not working you need to save your money."

"Molly and I are starting up our own web-designing business. Molly could do the bookwork and I could do the designs. That type of business can be done anywhere."

"Why didn't you just stay with Four Plus then? You did web-designing there."

"Mom, you know I wanted to get away from Dennis and his office. It always felt like it was his business and I was just his peon. This feels like home. Besides I didn't like what I was becoming in Calgary – just a fashion horse snob with no brains." Sophie smiled lightly. Her mother worried too much. "This way I'm getting some real money coming in. With my savings and the money I made from the company I can do things immediately. Dennis has hired a new web-designer so I won't get any more work from him."

Alice smiled and nodded. "That sounds exactly like my Sophie. Make sure you invest some. I'm not sure Sam is the best one to advise you, all things considered."

"No, I won't ask Dennis's dad. He won't even acknowledge my existence now." But Sophie didn't mind. Dennis's father had never been overly friendly even when she was with Dennis.

"You should turn my library into your office."

"I won't do that mom. You love your library." Sophie shook her head. Maybe I'll just use a corner of my bedroom. It's big enough. I need my computer and not much else. I'll drive to meet clients when necessary. Mainly all my contact is through the internet. Times change mom."

After dinner the air was crisp and cool already. Sophie put an old plaid jacket and her scuffed boots to go to the game. It was odd how fast she could drop back into comfort rather than style. And it was also strange how much better she felt, not worrying about her appearance. She ran a brush through her hair, growing over her ears and almost a bob now. Her natural wave was visible. She would just let it grow, then go to Leanne in town to shape it.

There was no heating in their old arena. It sat alone on the outskirts of town near the fairgrounds. Once the building was painted white, now it was chipped and sagging with a grey barn-board appearance. She wondered about getting town-hall to do some improvements on it too. Then she laughed aloud. Her dad always said *'Never take on other people's problems until you've solved your own.'* But it was so hard to listen to the advice when there were so many problems around she wanted to fix. She felt old, like her mother who had those same wishes.

She saw Millie enter with the baby and two little girls. She went to sit with her.

"Can I hold the baby?" A wistful question. Luke was bundled in a worn white bunting-bag. There was a cheerful blue bunny embroidered on it, looking new. Sophie smiled at Millie. "Do you embroider?"

"Yes." Millie smiled back, passing her the baby.

"Sit down girls. And watch Dominic." Janet and Julia were giggling and chasing each other, sometimes knocking into people as many came to watch the hockey game. No one appeared to mind.

Dominic's team was playing a team from Black Diamond. Sophie tried to ignore Jake when he came in and sat beside her. But inside her heart lightened to a glow.

"You came." She leaned over to whisper in his ear. "I thought you were working."

"I knew you'd be here." Jake gave her that beautiful smile that melted her all over.

Then he was silent, even as others around cheered and yelled to encourage the players. When Jake caught her eye he had a query in their depths. Sophie dropped her eyes to the wooden bench. Niggling doubts flooded within and she wanted to ask him a thousand question. Tracy not only went riding with her, but had also assured her she and Jake were still an item.

Dominic, falling as much as he skated, scored a goal. Sophie forgot everything except the pride she felt inside. Her boy, her Dominic scored a goal. Leaping to her feet, her yelp was louder than all the others. She was still holding Luke and rocking him. Luke opened his eyes and she was sure he smiled at his brother's success.

Glancing at Jake she tried to ignore the approval in his eyes. But she couldn't as bliss sliced throughout.

"Come have a coffee with me." Jake whispered in her ear as they walked out of the arena together.

Chapter Fourteen

The coffee-shop at the Esso was empty. The air was dry and stuffy inside. Sophie took off her old jacket and hung it on the back of the chair. Jake ordered two coffees.

"Do you want anything else?" Finally he looked up at her. Sophie shook her head. Now that she was home with her mother, she was eating too much. But her old jacket still fit so those gravies and sauces, mixed with Alice's homemade bread weren't harming her.

"I think I love you Sophie."

She was shocked into silence by his admission. She didn't know what to say. It appeared they were back to square one. Was Jake so undecided? *'I know I love you,'* just didn't sound right. It was too scary to admit it. It was her turn to drop her eyes and she could feel the heat rising in her cheeks. Think? He thought he loved her.

"Only think?" She whispered, almost to herself. "What does that mean?"

He was silent, stirring sugar into his coffee when the waitress brought it.

"I went riding and Tracy came with me this morning." Sophie's voice trailed off. It was quiet too long and that silence was awkward.

"I know." Jake continued finally. "Sophie, look at me. I told Tracy before the dance that it was over. She just... um... She won't... I don't know what I can do to stop her. She just keeps showing up. I don't know how to get rid of her."

Sophie giggled even knowing it was the wrong thing to do. Jake looked so bewildered and it was a though he expected her help. But what could she do? Should she know how to stop a determined Tracy? "I'm sorry. I know it's not funny."

"No. She scares me." Jake admitted. He flushed and looked down at his coffee.

"So what can I do?" Sophie finally looked at him again. Did he even want her help? "Should we start going out in public to show her it's over and the rest of the town will know? Because you *think* you love me?"

She wanted to take the words back. She was sarcastic and cynical again. Jake did not ever make serious decisions fast. She understood that, even though she was the exact opposite.

Turning to look out the window, she saw a truck pull up. It was a semi, not anyone from town. He got out, leaving the truck idling. A dull roar penetrated the silence. There was no snow, making the small beam of light from a street light look lonely in the darkness.

"Oh Sophie," Jake smiled. He took her hand. "Look at me. I love your directness."

"Well, at least you love something." She mumbled, refusing to look at him.

"I'm confused and even scared."

"I'll say." Sophie finally looked at him. "Okay, since we're being direct and honest, why do you *think* you love me? What changed?"

"Okay, damn it... I do love you, but I still don't think I should do anything about it."

"You think you shouldn't do anything about it? Do you feel obligated to Tracy?" She looked into his stunning dark eyes. Inside she felt a lightness invade but refused to allow it to affect her judgment. He was definitely frustrating. "Do you like this chaos? Are you a drama queen?"

Jake shook his head, as though he wanted to do anything but have this conversation. "Sophie, I'm scared. So petrified you'll make a fool out of me. I don't think I can live when you leave me."

"Of all the stupid..." Sophie yanked her hands away. The semi driver came in and she lowered her voice. She wanted to walk out and leave him to wallow in his thoughts. The sad part was she didn't know if she could live without Jake either. "It's your mother isn't it? You think I'm like your mother."

"What do you know about my mother?" Jake looked miserable and perplexed. "I know I'm saying this all wrong. My loving you is beyond thinking. I shouldn't have said that."

"I know the rumors like everyone else in town." Sophie's eyes darkened in sympathy. He looked like a lost little boy now. Was Jake living too much in the past? Is that what he and Tracy had in common? "I just know she abandoned you, or at least I think she did because she wasn't around when you were growing up."

"I've got over that." Jake smiled. But the smile was grim which revealed to her maybe he hadn't. "Yes, she abandoned me but I can't blame her for leaving Angus. She was so damned gorgeous Sophie. Nearly as beautiful as you. There were problems long before she left. Other guys... I wonder if that's what drove Angus to drink?"

"No, Jake that wouldn't be the reason. Everyone does what they want. And some blame others for their problems. If your father didn't trust your mother, than that was his problem. He should have done something about it not turned to the bottle."

"Wise and beautiful Sophie. You're right." Jake reached for her hands again and looked directly in her eyes. "So my mom left and my dad was a drunk. I can live with that today. Now what can I do about you?"

"Me? I think maybe you best learn to trust me. Before we go any further. I don't want a fling Jake. And I'm not your mother." Sophie tried to pull her hands away. He wouldn't let her.

"You're so stunning, I can't get you off my mind. I dream about you..."

"Is that all you see?" Sophie managed to free her hands.

She stood and knew she couldn't falter. "It's always the same. Jake, it's not love you feel. You want to take me to bed.

I've experienced the same thing from most guys I've met. I thought you were different. Apparently not. I think you best get your mind straightened up before we go further."

"Sophie, I'm sorry. Of course there's more than just beauty." Jake looked surprised. He stood to grab her arm. She yanked it away, stepping back. "I know you can do things. I've seen you with kids. I know you must be a good web-designer. I know you're loyal to your friends. But..."

"Jake there shouldn't be buts. You accept me for who I am or not." Sophie knew she had to do this regardless of how much it hurt. Jake still couldn't see things the way she knew she needed. "My loyalty extends past friends. I stayed with Dennis for nearly ten years and he was an asshole. Are you one too?"

And she left. Fortunately she had driven her truck to the Esso. It was dark and she maneuvered it down the road back home, hoping her mother was out. She didn't want to see anyone right now.

Her mother was home. Sophie came into the living-room to say a hasty 'hi'. Then went to her room and let her tears fall. Why did she love Jake? He couldn't see anything past her face, just like all the others. Normally she would never give that type the time of day.

Chapter Fifteen

After a restless night and knowing he's botched something special, Jake didn't know what to do when he walked into his run-down shack the following evening. How could he convince Sophie there was more than her beauty to love? She loved to laugh and was probably the most positive, upbeat person he'd ever met. He loved her laughter and instead of making her happy, whenever he opened his mouth he said the wrong thing.

But instead of going to her, he had to haul bales all day. He was exhausted when he arrived back at the shack.

His porch was dark and dreary, only unpainted boards, stained and cracked. Wind whistled through them and sometimes snow drifted inside as well. It was good enough to store his outside clothing and coats since he was rarely inside anyway. He didn't need a nice home. He needed to get the ranch running first.

When he walked into the kitchen, which at least had heat, he could smell roast beef and for a moment he let dreams filter in hoping it was Sophie. But Sophie didn't cook. His heart sank knowing it was Tracy. How the hell was he going to get her out of his life? Without her gone he couldn't convince Sophie he loved her. *'How do I love thee... let me count the way.'* He recalled the poem from high-school days. Maybe he should go to the bookstore, get it and hand it to Sophie without saying a word.

He sat down at the old wooden table, noticing it was covered with a new sunflower table-cloth. Dawson's marked oilcloth was gone. In the center cheerful sunflowers sat in a vase. Plates and cutlery and yellow napkins were appealing to the eye. The table was out of place with the plastered pink walls, rough and cracked too. Wainscoting reached half way up the wall. Chipped dark boards met with an uneven worn floor. Sophie would hate it and he didn't have the money to fix it either. '*Stop putting words in my mouth,*' he heard her voice clearly in his mind. Yes, it's exactly what she would say. Would she care what his home looked like?

"Tracy, I thought we discussed this. I thought we agreed it was over." Instead he had to deal with Tracy, yet again. Jake put his face in his hands and elbows on the table. He was bushed. He needed sleep. The roast sure smelled wonderful. He had only eaten some jerky today. His stomach growled.

"Well, you agreed but I'm not sure you really want that." Tracy sounded matter-of-fact as though she knew answers and he didn't. She brought a plate, heaped with roast beef, potatoes and Yorkshire pudding. His favorite and Tracy knew that. The few chunks of jerky he'd eaten while hauling bales didn't quite fill the emptiness inside. "Jake, I know you don't want to listen. But that bitch has you going in circles. Can't you remember what your mother did to you? Sophie will do worse, I guarantee you. Eat. You know you're starving yourself."

"Sophie is nothing like my mother Tracy. And you know it. It's none of your business." Jake looked up and didn't like what he saw. Tracy's face was screwed up with bitterness and envy. She wasn't trying to hide anything now. Why had he ever asked her out?

"Let's agree to disagree. But you mark my words, she will hurt you. And who do you suppose will be around to pick up the pieces?" She sat down with her plate and started eating. His stomach growled again.

"It doesn't matter Tracy. Regardless of what Sophie does or I do in the future, it will not change the fact - we will not be getting married. I am not asking you out again." Jake tried to keep his voice calm, but wanted to yell instead He wanted to yank on the tablecloth and smash all the dishes. Should he go around the table and just toss her out onto the hard ground?

"Nothing says we have to be enemies Jake. We did share good times. Surely we're adult enough to be friends? I know you have no intentions of marrying me."

Now, she sounded ultimately logical, making him look like a problematic fool. He looked at her again and nodded grimly. "Okay Tracy, let's be friends."

"Now eat." Tracy's smile made her pretty.

And he did because he was starving and hadn't eaten much at all in ages. Maybe he should hire a cook. That made him smile. He couldn't afford to hire enough hands, let alone a cook. Still, he felt as though he was making a mistake and using Tracy. It was uncomfortable and if he wasn't so tired, he thought he might well condemn himself for eating her food. He should take more time to go into Ryan's café and eat.

After supper, he wanted to go have a shower and climb into bed. Tomorrow would be another long day. Tracy however had cake and coffee ready for him. She set it on the tiny living-room coffee table and turned the TV on. He wanted her to go home but knew it would be churlish of him to kick her out after eating her food.

"I thought maybe we should cheer the place up for you." Tracy sat down on the couch and patted the seat beside her. "I made some curtains for the living room. I wondered if you could hang them. I'm sure Sophie will like it better when she's cooking."

'Get out, get out...' ran rampant throughout Jake's mind. He nodded instead. God, he was a spineless coward. There really wasn't any way he figured he could get rid of her, except throwing her out. He went out to the shed to get a ladder. The air was cool and refreshing. But he wanted to get those damn curtains up so Tracy would leave. Every time Tracy got her way, it was just another reason for her to push for more. He shouldn't have eaten her meal. He shouldn't agree to hang curtains either. Annoyed with himself Jake went inside and slammed the ladder down as he opened it. Tracy was standing holding the rod with the curtains calmly as though nothing was wrong. He wondered again how and what he could do to get rid of her. Even his behavior with Sophie, his glaring fascination, wasn't doing the trick. Tracy came back and treated him like her own personal slave.

Without concentrating, he climbed the ladder and reached down to grab the rod. The ladder teetered and he had nothing to hold onto. In an instant he was on the floor. Shaking his head, he tried to stand. He yelped in pain. He couldn't believe the agony his movement caused in his ankle. Lying back on the floor, closing his eyes for a moment. He tried again. He could feel the sweat formulating on his forehead. Throbbing from his foot shot through his leg. He laid back, closing his eyes. He had fallen off horses how many times and now a ladder was his downfall?

"Jake, oh my God, Jake…. Jake, wake up…" Tracy was on the floor beside him, shaking him. Her voice rose hysterically. He didn't wish her harm, he didn't wish her dead – he just wished her gone. Never, in all his life had anyone irritated him so badly. He refused to open his eyes and assure her it was okay.

But it was a mistake. She started screaming. Even when he opened his eyes she wouldn't stop. Tears streamed down her cheeks and she was frantic. He wanted to slap her. Isn't that what you did with hysterical people? But instead he tried to get up again. The pain was unbearable but less exasperating than Tracy's frenzied ranting and shouting.   "No… help… Jake… Help…"

Rover, his black and white sheep dog, came into the room and started howling joining Tracy's rant. The noise was deafening. He hobbled to the couch as Tracy sat on the floor screaming. She was in her own world. It was obvious she hadn't noticed Jake hobble to the couch.

Jake looked up and sighed with thanks to the heavens. At the door stood his beautiful angel. She was not screaming. She was just looking around puzzled.

"I think I sprained my ankle." He hoped she could hear him above Tracy's screeching. "Or maybe even broke it."

Sophie sat on the couch beside him and dialed 911 on her cell. She reached across to smooth the hair off his forehead.

"They'll be here in a bit." Sophie stated soft and gentle. "Here, I'll try and get your boot off and maybe get you some water to soak it?"

Pulling the boot off caused excruciating pain, but he bit his lip so he didn't make a sound. Tracy was still on the floor blaring. He hoped the ambulance drivers could give her something to knock her out.

Sophie brought him a basin of cold water. Setting it down on the floor, she sat beside him. "I forget whether it should be hot or cold. Let me know if it helps."

"I'm so glad you're with me. Thank you angel. Thank you." Jake knew he was grinning like a fool. He took her hand. The water on his foot and ankle felt wonderful. Holding Sophie's hand he realized the sound of Tracy's hysterical screaming muted. Life was good.

. . .

When the ambulance came and took Jake to the small hospital, Tracy was still collapsed on the floor. Sophie wanted to ride in the ambulance, but she grudgingly knew someone had to help Tracy.

"Come on Tracy," Sophie stood, shaking inside. She prayed it was just a sprain. The ambulance was pulling out of the driveway. "I'll drive you home."

Tracy's vehicle, a small blue Prius, was still parked in the yard. She made no protest when Sophie helped her into her car. Shuddering sobs wracked her body. She kept murmuring over and over, "Poor Jake, poor Jake..." until Sophie wanted to yell at her to be quiet. She didn't.

When she pulled up in front of Tracy's apartment building Tracy decided she wanted to go to the hospital instead.

Jake's x-rays revealed a hairline fracture. He would have to stay off his feet for at least a month. When he could see visitors, it was Tracy who rushed to his side, sobbing. Sophie stood at the door. She was conscious of Jake's eyes on her, not Tracy. She was also well aware of the worry in his eyes. Jake needed to be mobile. It was fall and too much work had to be finished before winter.

Chapter Sixteen

The moon lit up the ground below. Powdered snow replaced the grass on the slopes. The air was chilled. Now beside the campfire Sophie tried to warm her frozen fingers she couldn't even bend. If she put them too close to the fire they tingled so much they hurt worse. She put them beneath her sheepskin lined coat and rocked back and forth. Would she ever feel warm again?

Behind her a wagon with supplies sat, doing little to block out the cold wind. She couldn't find relief from the soreness and aches everywhere. She should exchange spots with Shorty's teen-age son, Brian who was driving the wagon. Then she disregarded that idea, thinking that the bumpy ride on the wooden seat of the wagon would only make matters worse.

"Here you go little one." Slim squatted beside her, handing her a tin plate of stew. Sophie smiled. She looked down at the unappetizing meat swimming in the sauce with carrots and potatoes. With only salt and pepper for spices, she knew it would be bland. "Sorry, I just couldn't move."

"You're doing great considering you were stuck in that city so long," Slim's voice had a humorous tinge to it. His leathered face crinkled. "Jake should really appreciate what you're doing for him."

"Remember you're not telling him." Sophie took a scoop of the stew and put it into her mouth. She was hungry. Her back still felt like ice but the front was warming up nicely.

"Why not? What's the big secret?" Skim snorted and sat down beside her. "There are times we gotta take help. And he ain't getting it from that useless bitch that hangs around his house. She can cook alright but ain't much good for anything else. He told me you're the one that saved his life. While Tracy was sitting on the floor screaming her head off."

"Saved his life? He said that." Sophie's laughter peeled out in the clear night. "Kind of dramatic. He only fractured his ankle."

"He said he felt like he was dying." Slim smiled at the ridiculous statement as well. "He's frantic with worry. You could set his mind at ease, by telling him. We're getting it done without him."

"I don't want his mind set at ease. Frustrating man." Sophie blurted out before she realized maybe she should be silent. "Sorry. He hasn't taken kindly to my help before. He thinks I'm just a pretty face."

Slim nodded, but didn't say anything.

Sophie realized it wasn't necessary to tell Slim about Jake's hostility towards her when she offered him money. Or how he ignored her suggestions to help. She could just imagine how upset Jake would be, knowing she was helping Slim and Boyd get the cattle down from the high ground.

She'd also made arrangements with Shorty, the rancher on the other side of Crystal Ridge, and he offered two of his men to get feed to Jake's winter feed-lots. Shorty also offered his son to go on the trail ride to bring the cattle down. She had Cal, Jake's other hand, cutting the oats to fill the bins with chop for the cattle. Shorty's two men were bringing in bales. Jake would be ready for winter soon. It crossed her mind, he wouldn't be happy. If she said anything he wouldn't agree. It would give his ego a real blow according to Alice. But things had to get done.

"Well, we got them all missy." Slim nodded towards the herd. "That's all them. And we should have them down to the feed-lots by tomorrow afternoon if nothing spooks them."

"We're low enough, I got Cal on my cell too," Slim continued. "Be warned, Jake is moving around with crutches. He'll see you."

"Yes, last I talked to mom she said he was starting to move around. The doctor said he had a hair-line fracture. Is it healing right?" Sophie whispered. She couldn't imagine Jake unable to move and do as he pleased. "Did Cal mention whether Tracy's been around?"

"Ah lassie. Don't worry about her. It appears Cal has taken quite a liking to Tracy. She's been inviting him to her apartment and cooking up a storm for him. But he's brooding because they had some falling out. Didn't say what it was. Poor Jake's probably living on beans and canned meat."

Sophie laughed then, her mind eased. She worried Tracy, with her cooking skills could wrangle her way back into Jake's heart. She continued. "No, he's probably eating better than he ever has. Mom said she'd bring him meals over. She's a better cook than Tracy."

"Love your loyalty kid," Slim chuckled. "Yes, Alice is one hell of a cook too."

They turned to each other as a wolf howl pierced the crisp air. It sounded so poignant and lovely to Sophie, but she knew the cattle might not think so.

"It's a good thing you were helping or we couldn't have done it so fast. And asking Shorty for some men was a God-send." Slim changed the subject. He stood up, throwing the remaining coffee to the frozen ground. "Better go check on the cattle. There is gonna be more snow on the ground tomorrow. Got enough blankets to keep warm?"

"Rover and Dog need a pat on the head too." Sophie didn't particularly like compliments, then accepted that at least Slim wasn't raving about her looks. She smiled. It was so good not to feel useless. "They did their job real well."

"Yes, we'll have to reward them with a good barbequed steak too when we get back."

"I think I'll sleep for a week instead." Sophie nodded her agreement. "Well, best get some sleep right now. It will be an early morning again. At least I see an end."

She stood. Her limbs were wobbly and filled with pain. But it was not nearly so bad if she hadn't gone riding this summer.

Who knew riding for pleasure was only practise for this long trek to bring the cattle down.

. . .

Frustration of inactivity ate at his stomach. Jake, always believed he was tough and now realized he didn't have the balls to even tell Tracy to take a hike. After ignoring him for nearly a month today Tracy came back. She was tenacious. He'd give her that.

She was puttering around the small shack, humming while she made him a meal with her usual efficiency. Why? Had the grape-vine in Crystal Falls told her Sophie was coming here today? He had heard that, so maybe Tracy had too. Alice told him something very vague about it. His heart leapt up in anticipation. He wondered where Sophie was as she hadn't come to see him even once this month. The desire to appreciate her and watch her stunning smile was a consuming need inside. He had cabin-fever badly and the winter wasn't here yet.

When he could finally at least stand with crutches, he watched out the window for hours, waiting for Sophie. Nearly a week ago, he caught a glimpse of her going into the barn and it was at dusk. A thin powdering of snow on the ground now revealed tracks from the barn, but even waiting at the window all afternoon, she never appeared for days. Going to the window again, staring at the sole light post by the barn entrance, he saw there were no tracks leading to the barn again. Where was she? How long did she stay out? He worried she was out riding alone. Then he worried she went back to Calgary.

Alice came regularly to help with the housework and to bring him meals. Whenever he asked about Sophie, Alice was non-committal. No, Sophie was still at home but out doing things. Sophie and Molly were starting up a business.

"Why doesn't she come to see me?" Jake didn't care if his voice sounded whiney or not.

"Maybe she wants to know that it's over between you and Tracy first?" Alice stated in a no-nonsense voice.

"Tracy hasn't been here for nearly a month." Jake pointed out. "Why don't you tell her that? I want to talk to her. Tell her that."

Alice just shrugged, saying nothing.

Or maybe she's moved on to another guy, Jake wanted to say. He scorned his cowardice. He had lied to Alice. Tonight Tracy was back and she was cooking him a meal. It was time to have another talk with Tracy. Even telling her it was over wasn't keeping her away. He'd allowed this to go on too long. He thought he had succeeded, now here she was back and pretending everything was the same.

Sitting down at the table, he ordered Tracy to sit as well. She was still puttering around, placing freshly baked buns down to go with the pork chops, mashed potatoes, gravy and applesauce.

"Just a moment. You want something to drink?" Tracy looked flustered and somewhat anxious.

"Sit." Jake knew he could procrastinate no longer. Even if he was about to chow down on her delicious meal. "Tracy, this isn't going to work. I can open up my own can of chili or beans. I don't need you here all the time."

"Are you suggesting your *cans* are as good as my cooking?" Tracy stiffened, looking petulant and hurt. "I haven't been here *all* the time. Only tonight..."

"No, I'm not suggesting that. You are an excellent cook." Jake realized this was not going to be easy. Tracy was like a child. You had to tell her over and over. "I don't want you here. It really isn't going to work. I'm not going to marry you."

He thought he was being too harsh. Tears welled in Tracy's hazel eyes immediately. She put her hand to her mouth, choking back a sob.

"Tracy you weren't here for a month. Do you think I starved without you? Now you show up today. Why?"

"I know Alice was coming to feed you." Tracy's voice faded. Then she continued, blurting out, "Cal was coming over to my place, then he stopped. And I don't know why. Do you?"

Jake wanted to laugh. His relief was tangible. The thought Tracy considered him incapable of eating without help, was overpowered by his stunned reaction to her words. Tracy and Cal? He better have a talk with Cal, hoping it was only some misplaced loyalty that kept him from Tracy. He would set the story straight. Jake had no interest in Tracy whatsoever now and would appreciate Cal… He cut his thoughts short. He better not tell Cal that.

"So what do you want? My advice?" Jake was in a great mood, but Tracy looked so serious.

"Well, we were always friends." Tracy flushed, looking down to her plate. "I don't know who else to talk to. You know Cal. What's wrong with him? It seemed as though he liked me, then…" Her voice trailed off, weak and faint.

"Maybe he doesn't know it's over between you and me?" Jake softened his own voice. She really had no idea about relationships. His heart was singing. She was moving on and that was good for his own relationship – the one he didn't have with Sophie yet. "Have you told him we just dated? Nothing came of it? And now if you still come here aren't you worried he may be jealous."

Tracy perked up at that idea. "You think?" Her eyes were actually sparkling. Perhaps she did like Cal for more than just as a man to feed. Either way, Jake wasn't concerned considering she would be leaving him alone. The pork-chops suddenly tasted so much better. He cut a piece off and stuck it in his mouth, enjoying the tender flavor.

"Maybe you should ask him why he stopped coming over." Jake added. It might be all Tracy wanted was a man to fuss over. He wanted to hug Cal and did chuckle, imagining Cal's reaction.

"You're happy now Jake but as your friend I think I should still warn you. I don't like Sophie. Every guy makes a fool of themselves over her. I was thinking Cal was seeing her too. I know she's been snooping around him."

"She has? What would Sophie want with Cal?" Even Jake's jealousy couldn't extend that far. Sophie wouldn't be interested in Cal. Then what was she doing? Or was this merely something in Tracy's strange mind?

Jake heard her insecurity. His mood fluctuated between anger at Tracy's condemnation of Sophie and wanting to soothe her worries. Regardless of who Sophie chose he never suspected it to be Cal.

Tracy was jealous of Sophie regardless of what Sophie did. If Sophie had to deal with that from school days it must have been hard. Now Tracy was questioning Cal's interest in Sophie. Why had he thought only a good cook and a girl who didn't attract other men, would make a good wife?

And at that moment he realized he had been ridiculous from the start. To condemn a woman because she was gorgeous like his mother, was childish and stupid. Sophie was nothing like his mother. He would just have to keep her happy so she wouldn't take off with another man. He understood her anger. She said she loved him and all he could give her was the same words other guys did. He could only talk about how beautiful she was. As though she was a painting or some valuable possession. He was assuming something without recognizing the truth. Now he realized he didn't care if his life would be no longer peaceful and calm. Maybe peaceful and calm was over-rated. It certainly couldn't take the place of a life with Sophie.

"Thanks Tracy." He smiled, genuine and real. "I think I understand too and I hope you can. If it's meant to be, it's meant to be. Sophie is not interested in Cal. And from what I've seen Cal isn't interested in her either."

"I hope you're right." Tracy still sounded insecure.

"I know I'm right." It was as though a light-bulb clicked in his head. He knew what Sophie wanted. And he knew he could give her what she wanted.

Chapter Seventeen

All good intentions fled into the air the following morning. Fury surfaced and Jake doubted for a moment he could give Sophie what she wanted. He tried to squelch his own self-doubt. The insecurity that he was really a wimp that needed looking after, incapable of making it on his own was foremost in his mind.

Jake was looking at his bank statement. He looked once, then twice. He walked over to the computer sitting on the little rickety desk beside the kitchen window. Tracy's flowery curtains hung dejectedly, looking out of place in the dingy light. Damn, he'd climb up the ladder and tear them down except for the fact ladders didn't mix well with his clumsy body. Incompetent fool. He suppressed that idea too. It was an accident, nothing more. But when he was upset he best avoid pushing his luck.

The doctor had taken his foot cast off yesterday. Six weeks had passed and he could walk on his foot again. The tenderness and weakness was a surprise. He was still limping. It was nearing the end of October. Today he planned to go riding and see how much work was left to do before winter set in earnestly.

First, he had to get his bank statements straightened out. He was two months overdue on his mortgage. When he checked - yes it was on the computer statement too – his hefty loan was paid in full. Wincing when he stood, he couldn't stop his anger. He knew exactly what had happened. Why would she disregard his wishes? She thought she was helping, but she made him look and feel like an inept fool.

Walking outside to the barn in the dim morning light, he breathed in the fresh, cool air with a feeling of liberation. He was mobile. He was active again. Saddling his preferred big stallion, he rode towards Alice's house. The hooves crunched against the frost bitten grass. Powdery snow clung to little dips along the path and on the rolling hills. The ground was hard, starting to freeze. Grass and weeds were both wilted and looking sad.

He noticed the construction immediately when he saw the Donnelly house. He scowled. How much money did she have? Sophie was both her mother and his new Fairy God Mother? He wouldn't admit the new roof and windows, combined with the freshly repaired and stained verandah looked great. Some of Alice's hardier flowers were still blooming. The sun was peaking up on the horizon. Welcoming light streamed from the windows.

Alice greeted him at the back door, letting him in. New cupboards with a modern island meshed with the wooden hardwood floor. It looked fantastic. Jake's scowl deepened.

"I need to talk to Sophie."

"She's still sleeping. She's..." Alice's voice trailed off and she clamped her teeth together before she turned to pour him a coffee. "Take it into the living room and I'll go get her up."

Jake obeyed and whistled when he entered the living-room. It was exactly what he would want himself if he could afford it. Leather black couches created an alcove around a huge coffee-table that looked like a chest. The fireplace was redone in grey blocks of stone. He set his cup on the coffee table, making sure he used a coaster so as not to stain the wood.

He couldn't believe his eyes when Sophie came down the stairs. Her hair, getting longer now was tousled and stuck up all over the place. She looked haggard and pasty. Her green eyes, normally flashing and clear, were blood-shot and dull. As she entered the room she reached up and tried to smooth her hair down and drew attention to her cracked, red hands. He noticed immediately her nails were chipped as well.

Forgetting about his bank statements, Jake leapt to his feet and taking her hands guided her to the black leather couch. He sat beside her still holding her hands and kissed the blistered, raw palms softly. "What have you been doing?"

Inside he knew. Inside he was crying. To think his belief that Sophie was just a pretty face was agony to accept. He couldn't believe how much he must have hurt this strong woman with his accusations and insults. Everything she did, she did for him. He felt humbled and awkward. How could he ever repay this woman he knew he loved completely? How could he ever make it up to her?

"Don't answer. I know." Jake still wanted to bellow. He looked up at Alice who entered the room with her coat on. "Can't the doctor give her some cream or lotion? Does it hurt?" He looked back at Sophie. She was smiling. Her eyes were brighter. Alice handed her a coffee and a jar of lotion. Sophie set both down on the coffee-table.

"We have a meeting in town. We've already started plans for Christmas."

"Oh thanks mom." Sophie yawned. "Some good coffee. It was so hard to ride all day without..."

"So you *were* out helping Slim and Boyd? You were out sleeping on the ground and riding all day. Sophie why?"

"She got home late last night Jake," Alice clearly didn't see any need to hold her words back today. "Yes, she was with Slim and Boyd bringing down the last of the cows from the high country. She went up twice. This time it really snowed yesterday up in the hills."

"Slim said they got all the cows in early yesterday afternoon. What were you doing after? You didn't get to the barn until late, after dark. And you didn't wait or come in to see me." He felt useless. He looked at Sophie. "I saw you last night when you put your horse away."

"She helped Slim and Boyd move the bales while Cal loaded the bins with oats." Alice supplied when Sophie remained silent. "Tell him Sophie. It's no sense hiding it now. Besides it's too late to change it."

"Well, I need to get to the meeting." Alice turned and went out leaving them alone.

Sophie looked guilty and pulled her hands away, she reached for her cup and cradled the warmth in her hands. She kept her eyes downcast.

"I don't know what to say." Jake cleared his throat. "Why?"

"Because you needed help and I knew you didn't have the money." Sophie looked up rebelliously. Her small chin jutted out. "Don't be angry. I wanted to do it for you. I remember helping dad. Fall was so busy. Slim did most the work."

"I feel like such an inadequate fool." Jake shook his head. Taking her hands, he brought them up to his mouth and kissed them with tenderness and reverence. "I will pay you back. I can't let you – Sophie you paid off the bank too." There was no anger left inside. Only a stunned, numb feeling as he tried to grasp the reality.

"Well, Mr. Willows was such a dink when I went to talk to him, I had no choice. He said you had fallen two months behind and he was going to foreclose."

Jake couldn't help but chuckle at her words. "Maybe he's mad because you didn't marry Dennis? Sophie, he's the only bank in town. I've kissed his ass a few times. Once I sold some steers I would have caught up on the mortgage. I'm not saying I don't appreciate it. I do, more than words can express. I'm saying I will pay you back."

"But he said he wanted it all."

"He says that every time I'm late. That's when I have to kiss ass and beg." Jake grimaced, shifting awkwardly.

"Well, now you won't have to anymore." Sophie smiled.

"Thank you Sophie. From the bottom of my heart I thank you. I'll do anything to make it up to you."

"I think it would be better just to do your banking in Black Diamond or Okotoks."

"I never realized you were so…" Jake's voice trailed off. The last thing he wanted to do was insult this delightful and surprising woman.

"Controlling?" Sophie giggled. "I didn't realize that either."

"You still look lovely, even…" Jake stopped. He assured himself he wasn't going to mention her looks. Insecurity reared inside. What did she want from him? "I mean, you're so competent, and you're such a big help. You know what to do much better than I do. Even with the ranch."

"Stop it Jake." Sophie reached up and stroked his jaw. "Don't sell yourself short, trying to please me. You're the second biggest rancher in the area and considering how you started, why feel incompetent? It wasn't your fault you injured yourself."

"Well, there's only two ranchers in the area… And it was my fault." Jake grabbed her wrist and held her hand to his face. Turning towards her, he kissed the palm with reverence. "I dreamed you'd come to cook me a meal. When I saw it was Tracy I got so angry. I was careless."

. . .

"Again with the digs about my cooking. Jake, I do know how to cook. Well, enough to get by so we wouldn't starve." Sophie flushed when she realized what she was saying. *'We'*?

"Temper tantrums?" She hastily changed the subject. "What can we do about your awful temper?"

"I have it under control Sophie, especially with you." Jake's eyes narrowed. He pulled her into his arms careful not to hurt her raw hands. "Sophie, I'm not a boy. I've looked after myself most my life. I don't need a mother. Save your efforts for Dominic. You're doing such a good job with him."

"I know you're not a boy." She whispered, very nervous. Jake was going kiss her. He convinced her that he was past the point of believing she was only a pretty face.

His lips touched hers, so gentle she could sense his fears, his worship.

"Now you can tell me how beautiful I am?" She whispered against his lips and felt the curve of his smile. Instead of answering his lips pressed more firmly and she slipped her arms around his neck, pulling him closer. Opening her mouth she let his tongue glide inside and answered with her own playful touching. Tingling sensations flooded her whole body and she pressed closer. The kiss was so intense she didn't want him to stop.

"You're beautiful. So, so beautiful…" Jake pulled back first. He was breathing heavily. His eyes were hazy with desire. He moved a little away, reaching for his coffee. He ran his free hand over his hair.

"Let's find a better place to make out than Alice's couch shall we?"

"I don't mind." Sophie was smiling, pleasure visible. "How about going out to my new truck?"

"Don't tempt me Sophie." Jake's devastating smile was in place. "I'll carry you out right now and probably break my other leg."

"Jake, stop making it sound like you were at death's bed. It was only a fracture." Sophie was teasing. "You only wanted a vacation."

"I have to get my palomino tomorrow." Jake was laughing. "Jed still has him. He's north of Olds. Would you please come with me later today?"

Sophie nodded unable to speak. There was such an intense look in Jake's eyes. He wasn't even annoyed at her paying off his loan with Mr. Willows. Worry eased from her chest.

Jake's voice was gruff. "I need to check a few things and then pick you up for dinner? Let's go to Ryan's and tell them the news? This week-end I'll take you into Calgary for a real steak and some dancing."

"A man after my own heart. A steak, a dance and... " Sophie was beaming.

"Other things too." Jake whispered seductively in her ear. Her imagination went wild. A night with Jake, the man she loved was too tempting. A lifetime with Jake would be paradise.

Chapter Eighteen

"A Christmas wedding and Pat said she can be my maid of honor." Sophie watched the sun creep up, promising a nice day. The sky was clear.

"Are you going to get married in the church?" Alice stopped and sat down at the kitchen table. There was a hesitant, worried tone in her voice.

"Yes mom." Sophie assured her. "We have to make sure we teach our children right."

"I'll get Father Bob to read the banns." Alice's eyes sparkled with joy. "Grandbabies, I can't wait."

"At least ten." Sophie teased. "And we'll need a babysitter for those times I go out and help Jake."

Gazing out the window, she jumped eagerly to her feet. "Oh look Jake's here with two horses. Guess he wants to go riding."

Indian summer promised a warm Halloween this year. Gold leaves fluttered in the wind, crunching beneath Sage's hooves. The path was powdered and dry. Puffs of dust circled the horses' legs. Ahead of her, Sophie could see Jake wearing his buckskin jacket. He was finally taking her to Crystal Ridge, the steep mountain, not the town. She was in 'no-man's land' finally. Memories flooded in. Riding up the backside of the foothill. Playing cowboys and Indians. Making a real campfire beneath the ridge. Hiding in the brush. She avoided the memory of her previous ride here with Jake. All those mysterious feelings she couldn't begin to grasp, yet wanted to experience. She wondered if he was remembering too.

Jake pulled to a halt. And turned to smile at her. Close to the ridge the rock was mainly grey or brown. She could see the twisted roots of brave plants, clinging to the uneven sides. She dismounted to gravel, scattered with quartz or crystal rock.

And because it didn't seem she would ever be able to keep her mouth shut, Sophie moved closer to Jake.

"Will you kiss me Jake?" She could feel the heat from his lean body and welcomed it. There was no need to be shy. The horses moved away to eat the dried grass and weeds. .

His smile snatched her breath away. She reached up to touch his jaw, caressing softly. The memory in her mind was as vivid as the time it happened so long ago.

"You rejected me, years ago." Sophie stated in mock reproach. She reached up to run her fingers down his cheek in a tantalizing motion. He took her hand and kissed the palm. "Do you remember?"

"Remember? It was the hardest thing I ever did." Jake's eyes were blazing with that same fire, she now understood.

"You shouldn't have. We could have saved ourselves so much time, Jake." Sophie slipped her arms around his neck, pulling him down to whisper against his lips. "Could you kiss then like you can now?"

"I suppose so," Jake shrugged in amusement. She felt his smile against her lips.

"I would have stayed instead of leaving."

"We're a good match and we always were. But you were too young. I had to let you go. Not now, I'm not."

Jake muffled her words with his exquisite kiss.

COMING SOON...

SOPHISTICATED COWBOY
Book Two: - Crystal Ridge series

- Raising in poverty, Dominic Reynolds is now a successful NHL superstar. He returns to Crystal Ridge, admired by all, except the one he wants, introverted Kate Bridges.
- Kate is hiding from her past in Crystal Ridge. Dominic, in the limelight, is just the type of person she has to avoid.

. . .

Novels by Mary M. Forbes

One Dance with a Stranger – contemporary western romance

Hawk's Gift – western historical romance
Alberta Wild Rose – western historical romance
Paradise on the Horizon – western historical romance

Made in the USA
Charleston, SC
05 June 2014